ROMANCE CONCERTO

A Novel

Nydia Hadi

AOS Publishing, 2024

Copyright © 2024

Nydia Hadi

ISBN: 978-1-990496-16-5

Cover Design: Jessica James

Visit AOS Publishing's website:
www.aospublishing.com

Chapter 1

Late November
Sweet Bubble Tea Café, Downtown Toronto

On a snowy Saturday morning, Gaby is sitting by the window in the Sweet Bubble Tea Café, enjoying her mango bubble tea while watching people and cars pass by Bay Street in the snowfall. She enjoys living in the moment and observing her surroundings, while listening to music on her earphones. To be specific, she is listening to the Chopin's Piano Concerto in E minor Op.11 played by André Gauthier-Lee, who has been her favourite Montreal-born pianist since she was a child.

Gaby has been passionate about the piano since she was five years old. That was when her parents signed her up for her first piano lesson. She continued the lessons until she was in Grade 10 at the Royal Conservatory of Music. Although, by the time she finished high school, she decided not to pursue a career as a professional pianist and instead pursued a career as an accountant. Gaby was never truly certain that she was *that good* at the piano. It took a lot to be a professional pianist. She ended up pursuing accounting because it was something she could do well and the job prospects were good. At 25 years old, Gaby is working at a firm as a senior accountant. She has just passed her CPA exam and got the promotion to senior position that came with the new designation. However, deep down, she knows that she will never enjoy doing accounting as much as she enjoys playing piano. Though these days, she only plays as a hobby.

The Chopin's music brings her to another dimension, in the same way that a strong and powerful emotion would, and so she does not realize that two people have walked up to her.

The tap on the shoulder startles her.

"What's up Gabs!"

She looks up to see Raphael, her big brother. Behind him, her younger sister, Michelle, follows. Raphael takes the seat in front of her and Michelle takes the seat beside her.

"Have you been waiting long?" Michelle asks.

"No, I came here earlier on purpose. To benefit from the surroundings," Gaby says, as she takes off her earphones.

"You are always so melancholic," Raphael comments.

The three siblings have arranged this time and place to discuss the important plans for their upcoming Christmas holiday.

Gaby Zhang and her siblings were born in Toronto from Hong-Kong immigrant parents who arrived in Canada around thirty years ago. Their mother is an economics teacher at a Catholic high school and their father runs his own law firm after working in the field for over ten years. Gaby, Raphael, and Michelle grew up in a nice area in North York. But now, the three of them have all graduated from university and moved out of their parents' house.

The three siblings catch up, as it has been over two months since they've seen each other. Gaby is typically busy working, and she often has to do more than eight-hour days, especially during busy seasons. Raphael is an emergency physician at one of the big hospitals in Toronto. He is usually on-call for night shifts. Michelle is a ballet dancer currently working as a soloist for a major ballet company in Toronto. With her schedule, Michelle rarely has weekends off after practicing late in the studio all week.

For the three of them to have gotten a month's vacation at the same time is a miracle in itself. Raphael had to beg his fellow residents to cover his shifts and begged his chief resident to allow him to take the month off. Michelle had to forgo her role in the upcoming nutcracker performance. As for Gaby, this is a perfect time for vacation. For the past two years, she has been working like crazy as a fresh grad staff accountant and was studying at least 15 hours per week for her CPA designation. Now that she has obtained it, this one-month vacation is going to be a great refresh that will help her decide whether she wants to stay in her current job.

"Alright, we have a big holiday coming up. I still cannot believe that finally the three of us can enjoy a holiday together again just like when we were still in school," Gaby says.

"Well, yeah, I truly look forward to this upcoming holiday that you are so excited about. Even though, could you explain again? What countries will we be visiting? And this is to attend whose classical piano world-tour concert?" Raphael asks. Unfortunately, out of the three siblings, only Gaby is passionate about classical piano. Their parents put Raphael in piano lessons when he was a kid as well, but he hated it. He preferred to play hockey. Michelle took piano lessons until Grade 5 but then got bored. Only Gaby continued her piano lessons until Grade 10 and still plays regularly. Every weekend, she visits her parents' house in North York to play the Petrof grand piano in their living room.

"So the tour will start in Singapore and then to Auckland, Geneva, and then New York. The good thing is, in every country, he will be playing different Chopin's pieces. And the pianist is André Gauthier-Lee. He is very famous. The reason we are going to follow him around the world for this tour is because this is his last tour before he retires," Gaby explains.

"And this pianist, André, is a piano prodigy. Gaby has been his fan since she was five," Michelle adds.

"Wait, did you say retire? He must be very old then. Since when are you fangirling a grandpa?" Raphael asks. He has zero knowledge about piano and classical music even though his sister is a piano player. For him, all the classical piano pieces sound the same. They make him feel sleepy. Sometimes, when his sisters played at a fast tempo, it sounded cool, but he still does not understand how people can synchronize the right and left hands, and practice the same piece for hours. It all sounds so complicated and too much work for him. He would rather read anatomy books or play hockey.

"No, he is only 29 years old, actually. He's the same age as you, Raphael. I don't know why he is retiring. He is so good. Even though the pieces he recently performed were either fast tempo pieces or sentimental pieces."

"I bet it is because he is still devastated with his breakup," Michelle says. As a ballerina, Michelle has a good sense of music. Although, when it comes to André Gauthier-Lee, she is more interested in following his personal life than his new compositions or new recordings. Rumor has it that André just broke up with his French cellist girlfriend, Charmaine, after 5 years of dating. Then, Charmaine went back to Paris. Gaby also follows Charmaine's performances on YouTube sometimes. Even though Gaby does not play cello, she enjoys listening to Charmaine. In her opinion, Charmaine is very talented and they were an ideal couple. She regrets that they are no longer together.

"Maybe," Gaby says.

"Okay. So I guess you two can attend his concert while abroad and I can go somewhere else on my own? I don't know if I can stand watching a piano concert four times during our vacay."

"Yeah that should be fine," Gaby says, although she is a bit disappointed. She hopes that the three of them can stick together while they are there.

"How about you Michelle? You can accompany Gaby to the concerts, right?" Raphael asks.

"Yes, I would love to watch André." Michelle smiles.

Gaby knows that Michelle is more interested in André's physical appearance than his piano skills. Even since childhood, André Gauthier-Lee has been very handsome. In all of his photos on social media, he looks very sophisticated in his tux. He is a mixed race of Asian and Caucasian. His dad is a French Canadian and his mom is Korean. So, André has brown hair and a Caucasian nose with small Asian eyes. He looks very exotic. Gaby followed his development from a boy then, to a teenager, and now to a full-grown man. André is of a tall and lean build. During his concerts, he always wears a white shirt, black pants, black shoes, and black suits that highlight his masculinity. However, no matter how handsome André is, for Gaby, his attractiveness stems more from his piano performance. There is so much emotion in his playing. As a piano player herself, Gaby is always impressed with André's flawless technique and his interpretation of music. His performances are very touching to watch. That is why she would like to enjoy them for the last time before he retires. Also, the reason for his early retirement is not clear. All of his fans were shocked with the announcement released earlier this year.

"So we will leave on December 1ˢᵗ, to Singapore, and then fly to Auckland, Geneva, New York, and back to Toronto for the 31ˢᵗ," Gaby explains.

"Great. We will be travelling across the globe and to four continents. I hope I can handle the jetlag," Raphael says.

Gaby only smiles.

'This is going to be a super exciting trip. With Raphael and Michelle, and also the last piano performances by André Gauthier-Lee. I can't wait!' she thinks.

Chapter 2

Late November
André's Residence, Downtown Montreal

André Gauthier-Lee moves his fingers effortlessly over the piano keys. He has been playing Chopin's Etude Op. 10 No. 1 for the past thirty minutes. Although, his eyes are fixed on the *Vieux Port* through his floor-to-ceiling window. André lives on the fifty-fifth floor of one of the nicest condo buildings in Montreal. He can see the St. Lawrence River frozen in late November.

Next week, he will begin his last world-tour, playing in four different continents: Asia, Oceania, Europe, and America. His retirement is not voluntary. In fact, André still enjoys playing piano as much as before. He never wants to stop playing piano. Piano has been his life. Unfortunately, however, his career as a professional pianist has to end. Other people may be confused. He made a lot of money from his live concerts, he always received a standing applause from the audience, people adore him, and he lives a comfortable life in his million-dollar Montreal penthouse. What else is missing?

At five years old, his parents discovered that he was a piano prodigy. Then, they ensured that he was learning piano under the best piano teacher in Montreal. Since then, there have been almost no days without piano. Piano has become his best friend. He won a national piano competition at the age of ten. By the age of fifteen, he won his first international piano competition. After winning the competition, he travelled around the world to give performances. Many world-renowned orchestras contacted him to perform with them. He enjoys performing for the audience. He likes to share the emotion of the music with the audience and to make the audience feel what he feels about the music.

Suddenly, his phone rings. He stops playing and looks at his phone. It's the buzzer for the front door. It must be Guillaume, his manager. He presses the button to allow him to enter the front door.

Five minutes later he hears a knock on his door and he opens it. Guillaume stands there carrying a pack of beer in his right hand.

"*Entre.* Come on in."

"*Ça va?*" Guillaume asks.

"*Ça va, toi?*"

"*Ben, oui.*"

Guillaume is André's manager, his closest friend, and is almost like a brother. They met each other after André graduated from the Conservatoire de Paris and moved back to Montreal six years ago. Guillaume is a year older than him and he is an experienced manager for musicians.

Guillaume examines André's face closely. His friend looks very exhausted and burned out. He is also a bit paler than usual.

"André, you shouldn't push yourself like this. Practicing is important but your health is more important," Guillaume says sympathetically. They sit on the big sofa in the living room.

"Oh no, I am tired not because I am practicing too much. I just started practicing thirty minutes ago. I have been busy with Gauthier Capital matters. We are in the middle of an Initial Public Offering right now. I haven't had much sleep," André explains.

Only a small number of people know that in addition to being a pianist, André has owned a private equity firm since he was twenty-three years old. Six years ago, right before his graduation day from the Conservatoire de Paris, his parents passed away in a car accident. He suddenly had no one else in this world other than himself. Not only that, his life pressure increased when his dad left him the majority of the shares of Gauthier Capital, a private equity firm with offices in Vancouver, Calgary, Toronto, and Montreal. André currently serves as one of the board members and as the major shareholder.

It's not André's personality to own a business without knowing how to run it. After moving back to Montreal, in the middle of piano performances, concerts, and recordings, he enrolled at McGill University to study finance. At twenty-eight years old, he has a master in music and a master in finance. What a hectic life he has. Running a firm as well as performing around the world.

"Well, okay. Will that be over by the time your tour starts?

"No. This IPO is a long process and it has just started. But I think I can manage my time between this work and my rehearsals."

"Alright. Don't give yourself too much pressure though. You have already mastered all the pieces anyway."

"Yeah, right," André says unenthusiastically. Both men crack open a beer and raise it before drinking.

"So, you still don't want to tell me why you decided to retire?" Guillaume asks him for the tenth time.

André does not answer at first. He drinks his beer and looks through the window. What a beautiful and calm day. Even though all he can see is snow everywhere, he does not want to ruin the atmosphere. But this may be the right time to let Guillaume know.

"You told me it has nothing to do with Gauthier Capital. You are not interested in taking over the CEO position either. Does this have anything to do with Charmaine?" Guillaume does not give up. Charmaine is André's ex-girlfriend, whom he met at the Conservatoire de Paris. They graduated in the same year and she came with him to

Montreal, leaving her hometown Paris. Charmaine came at the right time, which was when he was still mourning his parents' death. She was the only reason he could bear all the sadness. They dated for five years, but they broke up because Charmaine felt that he was too busy with his responsibilities and had no time for her. They parted amicably and she moved back to Paris right away.

Charmaine was the only woman André ever cared about. She was very gentle, caring, supportive, and talented. She was as devastated as he was when they broke up. That was the second lowest point in André's life after his parents' death. His condo felt empty without her. He has ended up working even harder than before after the breakup, as keeping himself busy was the only way to overcome his sadness. But his retirement has nothing to do with Charmaine.

"Since I came back to Montreal, I never rest. I work harder than before in everything I do; piano, finance, you name it. That's because..." André hesitates for a moment.

"That's because?" Guillaume is almost frustrated in his curiosity. Why can't André just be straightforward with him? They have been working together for the past six years. They have been through ups and downs together. Whether it was celebrating André's post-concert success, celebrating Gauthier Capital's new client acquisitions, or when André had a mental breakdown due to work pressure. André is a perfectionist and always has high expectations of himself.

Although Guillaume is aware that André is a very private person, Guillaume is not aware of all the problems he keeps to himself.

André starts telling him the whole story. Guillaume has never heard any more shocking news in his life. He drops his can, and the beer spills out all over the floor.

Chapter 3

Early December
Pearson International Airport, Terminal 1

The Zhang siblings are enjoying their drinks at the Beerhive at Terminal 1 of Pearson airport. They are waiting to board the plane to Singapore via Hong Kong.

"I cannot believe I will be having a full month without being in the ER!" Raphael says.

"Is that good or bad?" Gaby asks. She truly appreciates that Raphael and Michelle are sacrificing their precious time to accompany her on this trip.

"It's good, of course. But not when we return. There will be paperwork piling up. And I am going to miss the ICU rotation," Raphael says.

"How about you Michelle?" Gaby asks.

"I am okay. I need a break from ballet too. But not a month. So I will probably still be practicing during vacay," Michelle answers.

"Thank you so much for accompanying me. It means a lot. Sorry to put you in a difficult position like this," Gaby apologizes.

"Hey, don't worry. We also need a vacay and this will be a great trip!" Raphael says.

"Do you think we will have a chance to meet with the pianist face to face, Gabs?" Michelle asks. Even though Gaby has always attended André's concerts whenever he performed in Roy Thompson Hall or Koerner Hall in Toronto, they had never actually met. Before André's announcement of retirement, Gaby always thought he would perform forever.

Seeing as this might be his last performance, Gaby wishes that they can meet and chat, although it is unlikely. André is a celebrity in the piano world and Gaby would love to know what inspires him and how he practices.

"I am not sure, but I hope so."

"Hey, you are going to practically follow him around the world. Even I would be disappointed if you cannot get his photograph or signature," Raphael adds.

"It's not about his photograph or signature. I am more interested in talking to him and extracting what is on his mind. Why does he choose to play certain pieces? What makes him compose a piece like this and like that, and so on."

"Yeah, I am also impressed with him. I am sure he works crazy hard, practicing for hours and hours every day. As a performer, I can relate. It's a high pressure role."

Michelle is 23 years old and she has already been working for the ballet company for five years. In Gaby's opinion, she is still young and has a great career ahead. But Michelle is always worried that she is already too old in the ballet world and she is afraid that she will never be promoted to principal dancer.

Raphael and Gaby have always attended her ballet performances since they were in elementary school. Michelle is always very elegant and stands out among other dancers. She has a strong body and strong technique. Gaby was very excited but not surprised when Michelle was promoted to soloist. It is just a matter of time until she is promoted to principal.

Suddenly they hear the boarding announcement for the Cathay Pacific flight to Hong Kong. Gaby, Raphael, and Michelle gather their belongings and line up in front of the gate. They pass the checkpoint at the gate and board the plane.

They get the three seats by the window. Gaby chooses the window seat and Michelle chooses the aisle seat. That leaves Raphael in the middle seat and he is not happy.

Gaby looks outside the window. It is dark outside. She sees some people are down there trying to clear off the snow from the runaway. When the plane takes off, she can see Toronto is getting smaller and smaller. She likes the night flight because she can enjoy the night sky. She recognizes the lights from the CN Tower and financial district. She can also see cars passing by Gardiner Expressway. Only Lake Ontario she cannot see because it is dark.

"Uhh, ready for the fifteen-hour flight?" Raphael asks.

"Yeah!" Gaby and Michelle answer at the same time.

See you in a month, Toronto!

*

Early December
Pierre Elliot Trudeau Airport, Montreal

André and Guillaume board the Air France business class. Their flight will have a layover in Paris before heading to Singapore.

The flight attendant offers them wine after the plane takes off. André and Guillaume receive the wine and adjust their recliners. They have not talked much since their conversation at André's place last week.

Guillaume is still shocked with the news and he is not sure what to do. He looks at André. He seems relaxed now while enjoying the wine and the night view from the window.

Guillaume is the only son in his family. He always envies his friends who have brothers and sisters. When he met André six years ago, they became friends right away because they are both the only child and do not have siblings. Their relationship has grown beyond the manager-artist relationship. They are more like brothers. When André was dating Charmaine, they sometimes invited Guillaume. The three of them had a great time in Montreal. They went skiing and snowboarding at Mont Tremblant every winter. They often had a short getaway to Quebec City. And Guillaume's parents always welcomed André and Charmaine for thanksgiving dinner as they were aware that André probably missed his parents and Charmaine missed her parents back in Paris. Guillaume always accompanied André whenever he went on a concert tour. Charmaine sometimes came along too. They travelled around the world together and spent time sightseeing in the new cities they visited. When Charmaine left, André was depressed, and Guillaume could understand that.

Soon, André will leave him too.

Ah, he cannot bear this thought. He just needs to enjoy their last moment. Guillaume finishes his wine and tries to sleep, but he cannot. No matter how much wine he drinks, he cannot sleep after receiving the bad news from André.

"Guillaume?" André calls him.

"Yes?"

"I am sorry for not telling you earlier."

"It's okay."

"You know that I really appreciate you accompanying me on the concert tours right?"

"André, would you please stop talking like that? I don't want to think about it. Can you please pretend that this is not your last tour?"

Chapter 4

Thursday Afternoon
Marina Bay Sands, Singapore

Their cab stops in front of the famous Singapore landmark: Marina Bay Sands. The last time the Zhang siblings visited Singapore was fifteen years ago, before The Marina Bay Sands was built. The moment they landed at Jewel Changi airport that afternoon and along the cab ride from the airport to Marina Bay Sands, Gaby was actually amazed by how much Singapore had developed. It is super modern compared to fifteen years ago. Downtown Singapore is very nice and everything is very clean.

Marina Bay Sands opened in 2010. It is one of the most luxurious resorts in the world. The architecture of the building is unique. It consists of three towers with a giant ship-like structure on the top that bridges all the three towers. The Marina Bay Sands complex includes a hotel, a convention-exhibition centre, a mall and shops, a museum, a theatre, and a casino.

Apparently, December is very hot in Singapore. They stowed their winter jackets in their luggage back at Pearson. But their sweaters are still too hot for Singapore weather. The good thing is: no more gloomy winter like in Toronto. It's sunny and bright in Singapore, which is perfect for vacation.

They exit from the taxi, enter the high ceilinged lobby, and check in at the reception. Then, they go to their room on the 45th floor facing the Marina Bay and financial district.

"Woaah, the view is so amazing," Michelle cries when she opens the curtain.

"I agree. Good choice, Gabs. Thanks for organizing everything. This is a legit vacay," Raphael says.

"I am glad that you like it!"

They had booked a room with twin beds. Michelle and Gaby will share a bed while Raphael can have the other bed for himself.

They change into shorts to go out exploring. The first thing they explore is the SkyPark, which is the ship-like rooftop. On the rooftop, there is an observation deck and Infinity Pool that offers a beautiful city view from the 57th floor. They can also see the Esplanade – where André's concert is going to be held – across the bay. It is impossible not to notice the building as it was designed like two giant durians. On the other side, they can see other icons like Garden of the Bay, Singapore Flyer, and Singapore straits.

Gaby and Michelle cannot stop taking pictures and Raphael becomes the victim who has to take pictures of his sisters.

"We should definitely swim later!" Michelle suggests.

"For sure. I am in," Gaby replies excitedly.

"I will just watch," Raphael says. Gaby and Michelle know that Raphael cannot swim. When they were young, Raphael almost drowned during his first swimming lesson. And since then, he has been traumatized by swimming pools. The beach is fine as long as it is still along the shoreline. But swimming pool is absolutely not for him.

"C'mon Raphael. You cannot miss this. This is not just like other swimming pools. You can just be hanging at the edge of the pool."

"Yeah, maybe," Raphael is unsure. "Let's take a selfie, the three of us." Raphael changes the topic. They try to take several selfies but unfortunately they cannot capture the beautiful city view with a selfie.

"I will ask someone," Michelle says. She has no shame when it comes to asking strangers to take a picture of her. Among the three of them, Michelle is the most photogenic, feminine, and high maintenance. Her Instagram followers are more than ten thousand now and that is partially due to her promotion to a soloist.

Michelle approaches a Caucasian guy who is standing alone drinking his martini while enjoying the city view. The guy is wearing a short-sleeves shirt and khaki shorts. He looks to be in his early thirties. He has blonde hair and blue eyes, and his appearance is so elegant and cool. Gaby is impressed that Michelle is brave enough to ask this guy who looks like a model and a bit intimidating.

"Hi, would you mind helping us take pictures?" Michelle asks the guy politely.

"Sure!" The guy smiles and puts his martini on the ground while grabbing Michelle's phone. Regardless of his sophisticated appearance, apparently he is pretty nice.

"Ready? One, two, three." He snaps several pictures of them. "Please check."

Michelle checks the pictures enthusiastically but is still not satisfied with how her hair looks in the pictures. "Sorry, would you mind retaking?" Michelle gives her best apologetic smile to the guy.

"No problem at all." He smiles and retakes. Finally Michelle is satisfied. "Thank you so much, Sir!"

"No problem. Where are you from?" The guy grabs his martini from the floor.

"We are from Canada. How about you?" Michelle asks.

"Really? I am from Canada too! Which part of Canada?"

"Toronto. And you??"

"Oh I am from Montreal."

"Ah, nice to meet you. It's so nice to meet a fellow Canadian."

"Definitely! You guys are here for vacation?"

Gaby starts to respect this guy. He seems sincerely excited instead of doubtful when Michelle said that they are from Canada. Throughout her life, regardless of when she was in Canada or in other countries, many non-Asian people often gave her a confused look when she said that she was from Canada because she was not Caucasian. Or, if they didn't know that she was from Canada, they were making comments like "wow, how come your English is so good?" Apparently, there are some people who are still not aware that Canada is a multicultural country.

Before they have a chance to answer, the guy's phone rings and he answers in French. Gaby is pretty good with French and she can understand that this guy said something like *you are ready? Okay, I will be there soon.*

"Alright, I hope to see you around. Enjoy your time!" the guy says.

"You too!"

Gaby is wondering if this Montreal guy knows André. They are literally coming from the same city, Montreal. And Gaby guesses that by now, André should have been in Singapore. Today is Thursday and his concert is this Saturday. Gaby tries to get rid of that thought. Almost impossible. Also, so what if this guy knows André? He is also a stranger to her anyway.

*

Guillaume is enjoying the city view while drinking his martini. He is waiting for André to finish working. After this, they are going to go to the Esplanade for André's rehearsal.

While enjoying the view, he notices three enthusiastic people - not far from where he stands - who seem like best friends or siblings. A guy and two girls. They seem to have so much fun taking selfies. Suddenly, a memory of him, André, and Charmaine comes across his mind. It has been a while since André and him had fun like that.

Then one of the girls, who seems to be the youngest, approaches him and asks him to help her take pictures. He likes seeing their enthusiasm. And apparently the world is really small as they are from Canada as well.

He would love to keep the conversation going with this fun group, however, André calls him and he knows it's time to go. He says goodbye to them and heads back to his hotel room.

*

André has just finished reviewing the report in front of him. It is two in the afternoon in Singapore and one in the morning in Montreal. It is a perfect time to spend some quiet time to review the report while all the senior management at Gauthier Capital is asleep. But that means he has to stay awake tonight in case they need to reach him.

They have been busy finalizing the IPO of a start-up Tech Company where Gauthier Capital is currently the major shareholder. They bought this Tech Company a few years ago at a low price because the company had many internal issues even though it had a good business prospect. Currently, they have fixed the internal problems, and would like to sell this company through an IPO at a higher price. Even though André is not part of the management team, due to the amount of money involved in this IPO, he would have a final say on whether to go ahead with this IPO or not.

He has examined thoroughly this start up company's financial reports, patents, regulatory compliance, personnel, operations, business structures, credit history, etc. It seriously takes up a lot of space in his mind and takes much time.

There is a knock on the door and he lets Guillaume come in.

"Ready? Guillaume asks.

"Yes. Let's go."

They take the elevator down to the lobby level. Today, they will go to the Esplanade for the final rehearsal. He usually prefers to have the final rehearsal a day before the actual performance day. He will perform this Saturday but unfortunately, Friday is unavailable for rehearsal. So today is the only day.

Today's temperature is very hot, about twenty-seven degrees Celsius. Just like Guillaume, he also only wears a short-sleeved shirt and shorts. Last time he performed in Singapore was three years ago. He always likes Singapore. It is a very comfortable city. Their cab passes over the Bayfront Bridge and he can see the Singapore skyline and the famous Merlion and Fullerton Hotel on the left across the bay. It takes only three minutes by cab from Marina Bay Sands to Esplanade.

They enter the concert hall and André walks towards the piano, and starts practicing. Even though he has already mastered all his pieces, he keeps repeating and repeating the same piece until he feels perfect. He forgets everything about the IPO and just focuses on the piano in front of him. He spends four hours in front of the piano.

Chapter 5

First Week of December
Singapore

Gaby can say that this is one of the best holidays she has ever had. They have beaten the jetlag and explored Singapore. After they were satisfied exploring the SkyPark that Thursday, they continued exploring the MBS mall and had a great time shopping. Even Raphael, who usually didn't like shopping, spent quite some time in one of the luxury brands for menswear. He made the excuse that he was bored with wearing scrubs all the time. The mall itself was very cool because it was very huge and modern and there was even a fake canal on the ground floor that mimicked Venice like The Venetian in Las Vegas or Macao.

After shopping at Marina Bay Sands, they explored the financial district and did some sightseeing at Merlion, Esplanade, Fullerton Hotel, Raffles Statue, and Clarke Quay. Even though they technically could take the MRT (Mass Rapid Transit) to get from one place to another, they preferred to walk as they wanted to explore as many corners of Singapore as possible. In downtown, a lot of people seemed to be walking in rush in their business attire while holding their phones. Back in Toronto, she was like one of these people. But now, she was on vacation. Gaby forgot how to feel this free and positive. The tropical country was indeed a paradise!

On Friday, they took the gondola from Harbourfront Station to Sentosa Island. Gaby really enjoyed the gondola rides. The height was probably about 200ft above the mean sea level. Luckily, none of them were afraid of height. In fact, Gaby loved height. From the gondola, she could see Sentosa Island from above which included resorts, the beach, green spaces, a waterpark, and a theme park. She could enjoy the water view of Singapore Strait, which had many ships harboured there. The gondola rides only took about 15 minutes one way.

They spent some time at Sentosa Island's Siloso Beach, sunbathing. Actually only Michelle liked to sunbathe. Raphael and Gaby were not obsessed with tanning. They were more cautious about the consequences of the UV light from the sun. After sunbathing, they explored the island and then returned to the main Singapore Island by gondola.

They had lunch at Orchard Road to gather energy before shopping. They tried several local Singaporean food like Hainanese chicken rice; *Laksa* – which is spicy noodle served in spicy coconut soup; and *Nasi Lemak* – which is coconut milk rice cooked with *pandan* leaf and served with spices and meat selections on a banana leaf. There were some Malay Singaporean restaurants in Toronto, but none was as good as this.

After lunch, they burned the calories by exploring the Orchard Road from end to end. Michelle bought a lot of dresses, a handbag, and shoes. Gaby only bought a dress and Raphael was more interested in eating the ice cream sandwich sold in a food bike cart along the Orchard Road. Instead of serving the ice cream with cookies like in the west, here, they wrapped the ice cream with a slice of bread.

On Saturday morning, they were just relaxing in the hotel and swimming in the Infinity Pool. Raphael once again became their photographer. Gaby thought that it was an incredible experience swimming at the Infinity Pool. It was like you were floating in the sky, feeling close to the blue sky while enjoying the city view from above. It wasn't like any other experience in her life. She really regretted that Raphael could not join them and only enjoyed the view from the pool chair. She also saw him get into conversation with some pretty girls in bikinis.

Gaby cannot wait for the evening. It is the night of André's performance.

*

After the rehearsal on Thursday, André felt ready for his performance this upcoming Saturday. Now all he can do is just relax and do some light practice during the day and work in the evening. He has no intention in going sightseeing as he lost count on how many times he has been to Singapore throughout his life. Travelling around the world has been his life since he was fifteen years old. He has seen almost all the most beautiful places on earth. As it becomes part of his life, he feels nothing special anymore.

On Friday morning, he practiced from eight to eleven on the baby grand piano in his presidential suite. Now in the afternoon, he is swimming at the Infinity Pool while Guillaume is just relaxing at Spago lounge, also on the SkyPark floor. It has been a while since André could enjoy the present moment without thinking about work. He enjoys looking at the blue sky and the city view. He is never bored with this swimming pool and that is why every time he has a concert in Singapore, he always stays at MBS. He also swims at least twenty laps back and forth, alternates between freestyle and butterfly style, and only stops when he is out of breath and Guillaume calls him out.

"Time to get out." Guillaume says from the edge of the pool. Guillaume hands him the bathrobe. André has no choice but to get out of the pool.

"What is it?" André asks while wearing his bathrobe.

"You need to rest. You are working again tonight right?"

Guillaume is right. They go back to their large presidential suite and André takes a shower. After showering, André works until 2am that evening. He would rather do as much as he could today, so that he can just focus on the concert tomorrow.

Finally, it's Saturday, which is André's big day.

He wakes up early although he slept at 2am the night before. He walks towards the window and opens the curtain so that he can enjoy the view. At six thirty in the morning, it starts to get busy in downtown. He can see the Esplanade from his suite's window and he cannot wait to perform there tonight.

After taking a warm bath, he shaves his face in front of the mirror. André is not only perfectionist about his piano performance, but also about his appearance. After that, he takes the elevator to the fifty fifth floor to have breakfast with Guillaume at Club 55. The lounge offers a gorgeous Singapore water view.

"Are you ready for tonight?" Guillaume asks.

"Yes," André answers while eating his egg benedict.

"What time did you finish work yesterday?"

"About 2am."

"You were swimming for almost two hours yesterday and then worked for six hours. And that was during the day before your big day. Can you please make my life easier by managing your schedule, your health, and your life better?"

"Guillaume, this is not the first time I do this. You have known how I managed my time for six years now."

"Yes but you are..." Guillaume stops.

André looks at him. He knows what Guillaume wants to say without him finishing the sentences.

"I am fine."

"Okay."

After breakfast, he goes back to his suite to practice. He practices the scales and etudes to warm up.

I am fine...

Chapter 6

Saturday Evening
Esplanade, Singapore

The Esplanade Concert Hall is full that evening. The hall has a capacity for over sixteen hundred people and it is such a huge concert hall with four levels. Gaby and Michelle sit on the main floor. Raphael finally became curious and he bought a last minute ticket and got a seat in the balcony on the third level.

It is still thirty minutes before the concert begins, but most of the audience has gathered in the hall. Gaby looks at the program booklet cover that was distributed before they entered the hall. On the cover, André is sitting on the piano bench and smiling. He looks very good looking with slicked-back hair and a tux. His Eurasian face definitely stands out. It's not a warm face nor a cold face. He looks like someone who lives in his own world. He is very mysterious.

Gaby turns the booklet to the next page and reads the repertoire that will be performed tonight:

Chopin - Etude in C Major Op. 10 No. 1 (Waterfall)
Chopin - Etude in E minor Op. 25 No. 5 (Wrong Notes)
Chopin - Ballade in G minor Op. 23
Chopin - Ballade in F Major Op. 38
~Intermezzo~
Chopin - Ballade in A-flat Major Op. 47
Chopin - Ballade in F minor Op. 52
Chopin - Etude in C minor Op. 25 No. 12 (Ocean)

Gauthier-Lee - The Loner

The repertoire for the first concert in Singapore consists of Chopin's Etudes, Ballades, and André's own composition, The Loner. The Etudes require strong technique. These are not easy Etudes. The tempo is fast, mostly allegro to vivace. André's own composition, The Loner, is a combination of fast and slow. Gaby has listened to The Loner before. Many pianists compose pieces that require demanding technique but she feels that they are very soulless and very contemporary. She admits that she never understands contemporary music. But The Loner is unique. Yes, it also requires arduous technique but it is still melodious, even though the melody is mostly dark and sad. There is a story behind each of his compositions. So it feels like listening to romantic era music composed in the twenty first century.

Suddenly the lights in the hall are dimmed except for the spotlight on the stage, focusing on the Steinway and Sons grand piano. It is the sign that the concert is about to begin. Gaby is super excited!

The audience applauds and André Gauthier-Lee walks onto the stage. He wears a white shirt, black tie, black pants, and black suit jacket. His hair is slicked back just like in the cover. At twenty-nine, André looks very mature and professional. He is very charming but mysterious. He walks towards the piano confidently and smiles and bows to the audience. The applause just becomes louder.

André sits at the piano and begins with Chopin's Etude Op. 10 No.1 (Waterfall). Then, everybody in the concert hall forgets where they are. André's music is like bringing the audience to another dimension. His dimension. His world. His fingers are so effortless but powerful. His music is strong and thrilling but still flowing very smoothly. The audience is absorbing his emotion through the music.

Guillaume is watching his friend's performance from the VIP seat in the front row. He has been watching André for more than six years now. Even before he became André's manager. He is never bored with André's performance. There is always something new to absorb and enjoy. He also notices that André may play the same piece differently depending on his mood. Guillaume knows how much work André has put in. He works really hard and is very dedicated. Tonight, he is performing as brilliantly as ever. From his music and his expression when playing piano on stage, Guillaume knows that André is enjoying his own world. And André brings the audience into his world too. His fast-paced life as a pianist and as a firm owner. But at the same time, it is an extremely lonely life. These emotions are reflected in the Ballades that he is currently playing. It is supposed to be about a happy life, but there are still emotional challenges like sadness and loneliness.

André and Guillaume consistently travel around the world. André spent tons of hours of practicing by himself in his suite. He recorded and released new albums. And the only time he was not alone was probably when he was performing piano concertos with local orchestras. But because André travelled a lot, it was hard to maintain long lasting friendships. Moreover, all André's classmates from the Conservatoire de Paris were also pursuing their careers and travelling around the world too. So, André barely made any friends in either Montreal or Paris.

Tonight, André's performance shows the result of his talent, his hard work, his sacrifice, and his loneliness too. It shows in André's expression on the stage behind the grand piano.

Guillaume is proud of his friend.

*

André is finishing his last piece before the intermission. His heart is beating very fast. Regardless of how many times he performs throughout his life, his heart always races due to excitement rather than nervousness. He enjoys his surroundings. The grand and high ceiling hall, the audience, the spotlight, and the piano itself. He focuses on the music he plays. It's his way of communicating with the audience. He wants his music to tell a story. To make the audience feel what he feels. And he is successful.

After his last notes, the audience gives him a loud applause. He bows and then returns to the dressing room.

He does not realize he sweats so much. He is wiping his sweat from his forehead when Guillaume enters. Guillaume looks very proud of him.

"Brilliant! That was amazing!" Guillaume says and offers him a bottle of water.

"Thanks! Phew!" André drinks the water.

Guillaume's excitement does not last long. He notices that his friend is panting and out of breath. André looks like he is just exercising. Even though performing is also tiring, this does not seem normal.

"Hey, you okay?" Guillaume is worried.

"Yeah I am. I think I got carried away," André says.

"Does this have something to do with..?"

André does not answer. He sits with a hope that his heartbeat is back to normal.

"It's just an adrenaline rush." They sit in silence for a while. Guillaume is afraid that André's body cannot keep up with the energy level required for his level of performance. The only thing he can do now is to cheer for his friend.

"You have been doing awesome tonight. Keep it up and we will finish tonight's concert strongly and it will be memorable for the audience. Be strong, André."

*

The standing ovation lasts for more than ten minutes. And André ends up keep going back to the stage to give some *encore* or bonus performances because the audience never stops clapping their hands. Gaby is very satisfied with today's performance. André's technique is impressive as always. It was very thrilling to watch. The audience was worried that he would make mistakes with a tempo that fast, but he did not make a single mistake nor any asynchrony. Gaby cannot imagine how many hours spent on practicing to have a perfect technique like that.

When he played his own composition, it was a really sentimental and emotional piece. Gaby noticed some of the audience actually cried. And she realized that she was thinking about something sad as well.

By the end of the performance, André seemed to have given the most powerful performance of his career, until he ran out of breath. Gaby used to perform in public as well, although with smaller audience. And so, she recognizes the adrenaline rush that makes you breathe faster. That only confirms that André has given all of himself to this performance, which he filled with energy and emotion. What an inspiring performance.

Raphael greets them on the main floor right outside the concert hall.

"Wow, that was amazing! I think I changed my mind about classical music," Raphael says enthusiastically.

"It was indeed!" Michelle says. "Is he going to come out here, do you think?"

"Probably not. There are too many people. If he comes out, everybody will just chase him."

"True. Are we going back to the hotel then?"

"Yes."

They exit the Esplanade and look at all the beautiful Singapore night lights. After watching André's performance, even the night lights can make you feel lonely and melancholy. That is how powerful André's performance is. It can influence the audience's emotion.

*

André changes his clothes in the dressing room and wears glasses to disguise himself. He would love to greet the audience after the performance but it would take hours to greet the large audience, and he is too tired. They go through the back door and there is a cab standing by. They climb into the cab and close the door.

"MBS please," Guillaume says to the cab driver. They usually grab a drink somewhere after the performance. But not tonight. André seems worn out.

André does not complain. He does not need alcohol right now. He just wants to rest. He probably cannot work tonight as he is extremely tired. But it was all worth it. The audience seemed to be happy and entertained. He smiles to himself.

Chapter 7

Sunday Morning
Singapore

It's seven on Sunday morning. Gaby is already awake and cannot go back to sleep. She is still imagining last night's performance. It was so wonderful. She already misses her piano back home. She decides to take a walk outside and maybe get a coffee nearby.

She takes a walk at the Olympic walk. Once again, she appreciates the beauty of downtown Singapore. She can see the Esplanade from where she is standing right now. It was less than twelve hours ago she watched a performance that really inspired and touched her soul.

Gaby suddenly remembers that there is a restaurant with a piano not far from here. She saw it accidentally when exploring the MBS complex with Raphael and Michelle. She suddenly gets an idea.

In less than five minutes, she finds the restaurant that she is looking for, and sees the piano there. Perfect. It's still seven thirty in the morning and there is only an old couple dining in. She asks one of the waitresses if the piano is open for the public to play.

"Oh absolutely, dear. Go ahead and play. We always love to hear music," the waitress says.

The piano is a Yamaha baby grand. Gaby starts playing all the pieces that she remembers. Most of them are Chopin's. Once she starts playing, she feels like there is only her and the piano. No one else is there and no one else is listening. She even plays one of the pieces that André played last night. It's Chopin's Etude Op. 25 No. 5 (Wrong Notes).

She remembers how André played it so beautifully last night. She actually learned a lot from him. Until now there is a part that she feels like she played it so boring, but last night André played it differently and it created more long lasting emotion than when she played it. The good thing about Chopin's pieces is that there can be multiple interpretations on how to play the piece. The bad thing is, you have to be creative and sensitive. One thing Gaby knows that she is lacking is she tends to play the music consistently. However, consistency is not how you play Chopin. So she adds some rubato.

So she plays it how André did. The result is amazing to her ears. She discovers new ways of expressing her emotion through piano. Thanks to André.

*

André wakes up early that morning. Last night he was so tired and fell asleep right after the concert. However, today he feels more energetic after getting enough sleep. It's been a while since he slept more than six hours. He checks his phone and there are a lot of unread emails, mostly from Gauthier Capital.

André decides that he needs a new place to work other than in his suite. His suite is amazing and offers the best view in MBS. However, today he feels like he wants to blend in with locals instead of being isolated in his luxurious suite.

He gets dressed, puts his laptop into his TUMI laptop bag, as well as his wallet, phone, and keys. He exits from his suite and takes the elevator down. Once outside, he is thinking of any cozy restaurant or coffee shop that he can sit in to work. He walks around MBS and suddenly hears a beautiful melody. It is one of the Chopin's Etudes that he played yesterday! It looks like the sound is coming from a restaurant five meters from him. He enters the restaurant and looks for the source of that beautiful melody.

He sees a girl playing the piano in the corner. Throughout his career as a pianist, he never saw something like this before. She is a beautiful young Asian girl, probably around twenty years old. Her face looks so calm like she is in her own world with her music. And she is playing the same piece he played yesterday with the same style! The girl doesn't wear makeup and only wears a casual white blouse and yellow wide summer skirt. But for André, that even makes the girl and the music shinier. The girl is very slim but her hands are strong and firm on the piano keys. She definitely has advanced training in classical piano even though she's probably not a professional pianist - yet. She appears so calm, charming, and... cute. In André's eyes, she is so attractive with the piano.

André decides to dine in to listen to the girl more. He orders coffee and egg benedict from the counter and sits at the furthest seat from the piano so that he can watch the girl without anybody noticing. He quickly opens his laptop and suddenly feels very motivated to work. He is even smiling when reviewing his emails thanks to the beautiful music background.

*

Gaby does not realize that she has been playing for almost an hour. So she stops. And then she is surprised when the customers who dine in give her applause. She blushes and bows a little bit to show some appreciation, even though it was an impromptu performance. She feels the adrenaline and her heart beats twice as fast as usual.

She decides to order something because she is hungry and hasn't had breakfast. Also because the restaurant has been very generous in allowing her to play the piano.

"What an amazing performance, dear! Now you can order anything without paying!" the same waitress says to her behind the counter.

"Ah really? Are you sure?"

"Yes I am. What would you like?"

Gaby has never been this happy before. "Umm.. I'd like a coffee and a turkey breakfast sandwich please."

"That's everything?"

"Yes." Gaby smiles. Even though she knows she can take advantage by ordering more, she does not want to do that. It is not like she is a professional pianist or anything. But she is proud that she finally had a paid piano performance even though the value is a cup of coffee and a sandwich.

She grabs her coffee and decides to secure a seat first while waiting for her sandwich. Unfortunately, when she turns around, she bumps into someone and her coffee spills onto his white shirt, leaving a big stain on the front.

It was just a second ago she felt so positive after her performance, but suddenly she feels awful. Her face becomes pale right away. What is even worse is when she looks up and sees the unfortunate person who got splashed by her coffee.

André Gauthier-Lee.

N Y D I A   H A D I

André Gauthier-Lee.

Chapter 8

Sunday Morning
Singapore

Gaby is speechless. It was always her dream to finally meet face to face with André. However, not in this kind of situation. Splashing coffee! Ugh, can there be a worse situation than this? André looks as shocked as she is.

"Oh my God. I am so sorry. Really, really sorry." Gaby is feeling extremely embarrassed and guilty. She avoids his eyes and grabs a napkin from the counter instead. Without thinking, she tries to wipe the napkins over André's shirt as if the stain can magically disappear. Suddenly Gaby realizes her stupidity and steps backwards.

"I am sorry. I will pay for the damage." Gaby is still avoiding his eyes.

"Hey relax. Don't worry," André says. Gaby finally dares to look at him. He does not seem annoyed at all. His face is at least not as shocked as before.

"Look, I live close by. So, I can change this right away. It's not a big deal." André is pointing at his shirt. He smiles politely.

Gaby always wondered what her idol is like when he is off stage. Was he confident, mature, and professional like he was on stage? Was he actually full of himself and rude, or did he actually have a warm and loving personality?

The first impression that Gaby had was that he is polite and warm. But still out of reach. It's like this is someone with authority and someone who deserves your respect. But there is no sign of arrogance at all. It is hard to describe.

"I still feel guilty," Gaby says and looks to the floor. She knows that she is not making a good impression to André. He probably dislikes her now and there will be no opportunity to get to know him in the future. Hey, but at least he knows that she exists? She feels tears in her eyes.

"Well okay, why don't you grab a seat over there to watch over my stuff while I run upstairs to change? I will be back in less than twenty minutes. And then we can discuss how you can compensate." He grins.

Gaby cannot believe what she hears. She looks at him again and he still smiles but he does not look like he is joking. She looks at the table that he pointed out, and there is a laptop, laptop bag, and his breakfast.

"Alright. That sounds good!" Gaby says with relief. She feels like it is her lucky day.

"Perfect. I'll be back." Then, he walks away.

*

André cannot stop smiling on the way back to his suite. He keeps repeating what has happened between him and this girl just now. He has been watching her until she stopped playing and went to the counter to order food.

He then rose from his seat and approached her at the counter to talk to her. But he kind of didn't know where to start and what to say. It had been a while since he had a conversation with an attractive and exotic girl. So he stood behind her to think what to say while she was waiting for her orders.

And apparently, he did not have to say a word to start the conversation, since the girl bumped into him and spilled coffee on his shirt. He was shocked because the coffee was so hot and it burned his chest. Moreover, that was his favourite white shirt. If she didn't play the piano so well, he would probably have been annoyed. But for some reasons he was not annoyed at all and the girl seemed to be more in distress than him.

In the elevator, he replayed the girl's performance. She definitely possesses talent. She has a great musicality. The technique requires some work but with her strong hands, it is very possible. André feels like he has just found a hidden diamond that needs to be sharpened, but he is confident that it could be done.

*

Gaby does not know whether this is good luck or bad luck. She sits at André's seat. His laptop and unfinished breakfast are on the table. She still cannot believe what has happened. She finally stood face to face with André and they talked. What will happen after he returns? He mentioned about compensation. Damn. That sounds serious.

What should she do? Should she tell him that she is his fan? Should she tell him that she followed him across the globe just to watch his last performances? Would that make her look easy? But talking to him like this is only a once in a lifetime chance, should she just say it all?

In less than fifteen minutes, André returns in a new blue shirt. The sleeves are folded to his elbows. Gaby now notices that he looks so perfect. Even though this time he wears casual shorts, he looks as gorgeous as when he wears a formal suit during his performance. Different type of gorgeous. This time his bang falls onto both sides of his forehead instead of slicked back like during his concert yesterday.

"Thank you for watching over my stuff. It is much appreciated," André says. He sits in front of her. She cannot believe that she sits in front of one of the most famous pianists in the world.

"No problem," Gaby says. "Let's hear how I can compensate you."

"Oh yes. Actually I have been listening to you playing piano for some time. That was beautiful. How long have you been playing piano?" André asks.

Gaby started to feel relaxed one second ago but now, she feels tense again. Oh no! A brilliant pianist like him has just listened to her performance! What could be more embarrassing?

"Oh no. I know it was so bad. Please forget about it." Gaby blushes.

"No, no. Why? It was beautiful. I was impressed. I am assuming you are a piano student? Which university do you attend?"

"I am not a piano student. I am actually an accountant. But I took music lessons since I was five years old, until Level 10 at the Royal Conservatory in Toronto. I live there."

"Oh you are from Canada? Me too. I am from Montreal."

"Oh, I know."

"You know?"

Gaby cannot hide this anymore. "Well, I know who you are. You are André Gauthier-Lee. One of the best pianists in the world."

André looks surprised. "Thank you. You know who I am but I don't know you. What is your name?"

"Gabrielle. You can call me Gaby."

"Nice meeting you, Gaby. As I said, I enjoyed your performance. It was really good."

"Well, compared to a pianist like you, it was so embarrassing. So amateur."

"It is not a fair comparison. I have been playing piano my whole life. I do this for a living. And I got more music education than you."

"Yeah, I guess you are right."

"So what brings you to Singapore, Gaby?"

"Oh hmm..." Gaby hesitates. Would it be creepy to tell him that she followed him all the way from Canada to Singapore and other parts of the world just to see his concerts?

"Well actually I came to Singapore to enjoy your performance. I know this sounds creepy, but I am not stalking you or anything. It's just I have been enjoying your performances ever since I was a kid. And whenever you performed in Toronto, I always attended and enjoyed it. And I heard the news that you will be retiring soon and that's why I don't want to miss your last performances." Gaby cannot look into his eyes. She just looked at her lap while talking.

"Really? Wow, thank you Gaby. I am very honored."

"You don't think I am creepy at all?"

"No, of course not. If there is a pianist that I look up to and he is giving his last performances, I would come too, even though I have to cross the globe." André smiles again. Gosh, he is so good looking.

"So did you attend my concert yesterday? Do you have any feedback?" André asks.

"Yes. I really enjoyed it. It was very beautiful. I tried to play the way you played just now. But I think my skills cannot keep up yet. I like your interpretation of Chopin's pieces. It looks like you know how to create the right impression at the right time. I also like the composition that you wrote. There is a powerful emotion in it."

"Thank you again for your compliment. It means a lot to me. I really like Chopin. I feel like I can relate to him. And all my compositions are inspired by him."

"I can see that."

"So my next performance will be in Auckland this Saturday, and then Geneva and my last concert will be in New York. Are you coming too?"

Now Gaby really feels like a stalker. "To be honest, yes. But as I said, I am not stalking. I admit that I am a big fan of yours. Also, I think of this like a vacation too. My brother and sister are coming with me for the whole trip. So this is like enjoying your performances while enjoying vacation with my family." Gaby realizes that she is a bit defensive.

"Hmm, interesting. If that is the case, I have just found a way to ask for compensation from you."

"What? How?"

"For my next performances, do you want to perform together with me on stage?"

Gaby is not sure if today is real or it is a dream.

Chapter 9

Sunday Afternoon
Singapore

On the way to Changi Airport, André cannot believe what has just happened. He cannot stop thinking about Gaby. Her amazing piano performance for someone without a music degree, her knowledge and love of classical piano, and her loyalty to attend his last concerts. She is one of a kind.

They talked for more than two hours. First, they discussed her music education in more detail, such as what pieces she has been playing, and how many public performances she has had. Just like him, her favourite composer is Chopin and number two is Liszt. She has some public performance experiences but they were limited to the concerts held by the Royal Conservatory of Music for its students. She has joined some local competitions before and the best outcome she has ever had was passing stage two of the competition. Those experiences are more than enough for André to bring her to the stage. André has heard her playing before and he has high confidence in her.

When André asked her whether she wanted to perform with him, Gaby clearly was shocked.

"What? You want me to perform with you on stage?"

"Exactly."

"But I am not a pianist. I... This is crazy."

"You have performed right there just now." André pointed out the piano in the corner.

"Yes, but that was different. Here we are talking about your performance where people pay to watch. They surely expect a professional."

"I can always bring guest performers. Okay, how about we do a duet first? Say for this upcoming Saturday performance in Auckland Town Hall."

"I am not sure. I don't think I am ready."

"You will never be ready if you don't push yourself. Is there any piano four-hand or duet piece that you remember? It doesn't have to be the advanced level one. Just pick the one you are comfortable and ready to perform."

"Actually there is. But this is unlike your usual genre like Chopin or Liszt."

"That's fine. Which one is it?"

"Are you familiar with The Entertainer by Scott Joplin? That is the only piano with four hands that I usually practice." Gaby liked this piece because it was very fun to play. She had tried to play it with some friends. But even though she had no one to play with, she still practiced the piece.

"Yes I am. I played that piece a long time ago. So I will have to refresh my skills on that. Let's perform that." Gaby couldn't believe that André had just agreed to perform a piece that she chose. A world-renowned pianist followed her silly wish!

"What? Are you serious? For this Saturday?"

"Yes."

"It's less than a week! I don't have access to a piano to practice."

"Don't worry. If you have all day access to a piano until this Saturday, will you do it?"

"Err.. maybe. But how?"

"When are you departing for Auckland?"

"Tomorrow morning."

"I see. Taking into account the flight hours and time difference, you will lose a day. So, we can practice together starting Tuesday morning. And where are you staying?"

"Pullman."

"Okay, I will be staying at Sofitel. There will be a piano in my suite. And you are welcome to come and play at any time. I can book another room for you at Sofitel as well. Just let me know what you would prefer."

Was he talking about logistics? This must have been serious. She hoped that this was not a dream. Performing her favourite piano four hand piece with André on stage!

"Okay. But please consider this. This piece is not like your regular repertoire. Are you okay with this?"

"Yes. I always add one or two surprise pieces for my audience. This is a perfect piece."

"Alright. When are you leaving for Auckland?"

"Tonight. Let's exchange phone number and email, send me the music sheet with the arrangement version that you usually played, and meet up at my suite on Tuesday morning?"

"Sure." They exchanged numbers and email addresses. This was another dream that came true for Gaby. André just gave her his personal phone number and email address. Just like that!

"Okay. I believe you just compensated me for spilling coffee on my shirt."

Guillaume notices that his friend looks happier than usual. "You are smiling to yourself. Did something happen?" Guillaume asks.

André turns his gaze from the cab window to Guillaume. "Yes. I met a girl from Canada this morning. From Toronto. I heard her playing piano and she was very good."

"Oh really? I guess there are so many Canadians in Singapore. I met three Canadians on the SkyPark rooftop a few days ago too."

"Did you get their names?"

"No unfortunately. You called me before I got a chance to ask."

André remembers Gaby said that she travels with her brother and sister. "Were they two girls and one guy?"

"Yes! How do you know that?"

"Asians?"

"Yes again." Then André describes Gaby's physical appearance to Guillaume.

"Yes, I think she is one of them."

"Wow. What a coincidence. Gaby told me that they are here to watch my concert. And they will also fly to Auckland tomorrow morning. Can you believe that?"

"Really? Look at you André. You have dedicated fans. I am so happy for you."

André also told Guillaume that he is inviting Gaby to perform together with him on stage. "She definitely has talent. And we will be performing a piano duet this Saturday. We will be practicing together starting on Tuesday. I hope you don't mind."

"I don't mind at all. I trust your judgement. And it is always good to have a surprise during a concert."

"I agree."

*

On their final night in Singapore, Gaby, Raphael, and Michelle are sitting in the Ce La Vi club lounge at the SkyPark. Gaby has just recounted what happened this morning with André.

"Gabs, I am so speechless. I cannot imagine a better scenario than this!" Michelle says excitedly.

"Me too. This is so awesome, Gabs. Remember that you always wanted to meet him. Now, not only you have met him, but also you will be practicing together and get on stage with him!" Raphael adds.

"I know, right!"

"And you were so lucky that you played that piano at the right time. He got a chance to watch your performance."

"Aw, I am not proud of that part, you know. I am sure he must have thought I was such an amateur."

"If that was the case, he would not ask you to perform with him. And he would probably be mad that you spilled coffee on him," Raphael says.

"True."

"Anyway, we have to celebrate this. Cheers!" Michelle raises her glass. Gaby and Raphael do the same. Tonight feels more beautiful than ever. They sit on the patio overlooking Singapore at night. The city lights are very beautiful and the jazz music playing in the background is very calming. Today is one of the best days in her life. She tries to enjoy the ambience. She had a great time in Singapore and she definitely wants to come back again someday.

"So what else did you and André talk about? Was it just music related?" Raphael asks.

"Yeah, mostly about music. What else would you expect?" Gaby replies.

"I don't know. Are you only interested in him as a pianist?" Raphael continues.

"I think I know where this conversation will go. First of all, yes I am interested in him because he plays piano so well. So I noticed his playing first before his face. But at the same time, I also find him physically very attractive to be honest." Gaby is very open talking about her feelings to Raphael and Michelle and vice versa. Currently, the three of them are single. But they know each other's crushes and exes. Raphael used to be a player. He dated so many girls in the past without being serious. But now at 29 and due to work schedule, he has less time to date. But, he does not want to commit yet. He enjoys casual dating but not as much as he used to. Michelle also has a lot of fans. However, she just does not have time to date because of her schedule. Practicing every day and performing on the weekends. Many other fellow company members are actually chasing her but no one has impressed her yet.

Gaby herself has only dated once during high school, and it only lasted six months. Other than that, many guys expressed their interest in her but she was not interested. Not because they were not attractive, but simply because she enjoyed being single. She only thought of the guys who had been chasing her as friends. One day, a guy whom she had rejected asked her, is he not her type? She was not sure what to say. She didn't even have any particular type. If she can describe her ideal type, it would be... André Gauthier-Lee? Is he the reason why she is not interested in anyone? Because she always compares them with André?

"So you only have a crush on him?" Raphael asks.

"Yes I think so."

"What about André? Do you think he is attracted to you?" Michelle asks.

"Oh I am pretty sure, no. He is famous, Michelle. I am just an ordinary girl."

"I have to disagree. I think you cut yourself short there. Tell us more, did he flirt with you at all?" Raphael keeps fishing.

"Not that I am aware of. He is very formal and straightforward. And he is very hard to read too. That mysterious guy."

"Okay. You said you guys will be busy for the next few days practicing together right? I will be curious to see how this will end." Raphael smiles.

Chapter 10

Tuesday Morning
Auckland

It is seven in the morning, and Gaby is getting ready in her room. They landed in Auckland at ten last night after a long direct flight from Singapore. She texted André right after she landed.

10:05pm:

Hi André, I have just landed in Auckland. What time do we want to meet tomorrow?

10:10pm:

Hi Gaby, you can start anytime you want. I will be in my suite the whole day. Let me know what time you are going to come by and I will send someone to pick you up at Pullman. Thanks.

10:12pm:

How about 8:00am?

10:13pm:

That works. See you tomorrow.

So, they agreed to meet for practice. This may be a one-time life opportunity and she does not want to screw up. She wants to show André that she takes this seriously.

She did not bring that many clothes on vacation. So, she decides to wear a green blouse and her jeans. She makes sure her appearance is presentable, especially when meeting her favourite pianist. Not too much, but respectful.

At ten to eight, she is ready in the Pullman lobby. She would be lying if she said she was not nervous. What if André changes his mind after hearing her playing? What if she cannot play well in front of André? It has been a while since she performed in public other than yesterday. But yesterday she played purely for fun, not to perform. It's a different thing. If she knew that André was watching, she probably would be nervous.

Then, a black Mercedes stops in front of the lobby. Somebody gets out of the car. Hey, he looks familiar!

"Gaby?" The guy asks.

"Yes! We have met before. At the SkyPark."

"Yes. I am André's manager. My name is Guillaume." They shake hands.

"What a small world. I wouldn't expect."

"Me too. Let's go."

On the way to Sofitel, Gaby looks around the city from the car window. This is her first time in New Zealand. Last night when she arrived, she could not see the city clearly, because it was already dark.

Auckland is more beautiful and more crowded than she imagined. Although, it is definitely slower paced than Toronto or Singapore. They drive around the downtown area and there are a combination of old and antique buildings as well as high-rise buildings. It is a nice city to walk around. They pass Queen Street, which is the most famous street in Auckland, like Yonge Street in Toronto. The shops and restaurants look very tempting. She is hoping that she can explore the city with Raphael and Michelle later on. On her right is the harbour front. She can see a lot of ferries and the view is amazing. She also catches a glimpse of the Sky Tower on her left. It reminds her of the CN Tower in Toronto.

"First time in Auckland?" Guillaume opens the conversation.

"Yes. How about you?"

"Fifth time."

They start to chat casually. Guillaume is very friendly and easy to talk to. He asks her about her flight yesterday, and whether she still has jet lag or not.

"I think I should be fine. This opportunity is more important than jetlag."

"True. André is a very hardworking and disciplined musician. He has a high standard for himself. He will appreciate that you are willing to start practicing so early. It shows dedication."

"Thank you. Yeah, I am nervous like hell. I am not a pianist at all. I don't have a music degree whatsoever. I don't know why André asked me to perform with him."

"He said you are talented. So don't doubt yourself. Just be confident."

"I will, thanks." Gaby feels happy when she hears that André thinks she has a talent.

Guillaume knocks on the door of the Opera Suite. Then the door is opened and André appears in front of them.

"Come on in."

André looks as good as usual. He wears white shirt and jeans. He seems ready to accept a guest. The opera suite is amazing. The interior is done in a French style. Everything in this room is very elegant. And the view is directly to the harbour. From the big window, Gaby can see the water and the ferries. She can also see the luxurious condos along the harbour and a nice downtown view.

"How are you, Gaby?"

"I am good, thanks. How are you?"

"Good, thanks. Thank you for coming very early. Have you had breakfast yet?"

"I have not. But I am not hungry though."

"Trust me, you will be. Let's have a breakfast first."

The dining table could fit eight people. Wow. The three of them have a French breakfast. Gaby feels relieved when she finally drinks a cup of coffee.

"So Gaby, you have met Guillaume, my manager. We have been working together for six years."

"Cool. Yes, we chatted a little bit on the way here."

"Do you speak French by any chance?" André asks.

"Oh yes, I can speak and I can understand French. I went to a French immersion school," Gaby says in French. She is excited to finally able to practice her French.

"Wow, impressive. So would you mind if Guillaume and I are talking in French from time to time? French is our first language." André speaks in French.

"Absolutely not. Go ahead," Gaby replies. André and Guillaume speak Quebec French. Gaby is familiar with both Quebec French and the Metropolitan French spoken in France as she used to have French teachers from both Quebec and France. Although when she speaks French, her accent is probably more like Metropolitan France mixed with English accent. Quebeckers often glide the vowels and sometimes they pronounce *d* as *dz* and *t* as *ts*. Also, they often add a lot of là in the sentences. Even though it makes it harder to understand, Gaby finds it very exotic.

From that moment on, they mix English and French in their conversation. They chat casually during breakfast.

After breakfast, they go straight to the piano. André opens the baby grand piano lids.

"Here you go. I have printed the music sheet. Feel free to practice by yourself. Call me up once you are ready. And please don't rush. We have plenty of time." André smiles.

"Sure. Thanks."

And then André just sits on the couch beside the piano. She feels like he is her piano teacher who observes her play. André probably senses her nervousness, so he grabs his laptop and starts working on it. Gaby has no idea what André is doing.

She pretends that he is not there and starts practicing her scales and arpeggios. She tries to make her fingers relax. Because the piece that she will play with André also requires speed but lightness at the same time. After about twenty minutes, she finishes the scales and moves on to the actual piece itself.

"André?"

"Yes?" He raises his head from his laptop.

"Have you decided which part you are going to play? The first or second piano?

"Which one are you more comfortable playing?"

"Second." Gaby chooses to play safe. For this piece, the second piano is the harmony while the first piano is the melody. The first piano is much more challenging and the success of the performance will depend on it."

"Are you sure? I don't mind playing the first piano. However, I want to give you the opportunity to take a lead on this piece. What do you think? Do you want to try playing the first piano?" André asks.

"Okay. I will try." Gaby decides to take the challenge.

Gaby likes working with him already. André pushes her to step out of her comfort zone. It shows that he trusts her. Also, he takes the initiative and gives her the bigger picture plan, but he never micromanages or is picky. He gives her autonomy. For example, he asked her to perform with him, but he let her choose her piece. He decided that they would practice on Tuesday, but he let her decide the time. She feels like they will be working together very well.

She starts to play her part. Slow at first but then by the time she plays it for the third time, she adjusts the speed to the actual tempo required. Twenty minutes later she is ready.

"André, I am ready."

"Okay great." He closes his laptop, gets up from the couch, and sits next to her on the piano bench. Gaby notices that he smells really good. She realizes that they are sitting very close to each other. That is the closest distance between them. Their arms and hips brush each other's.

Then they start playing.

Gaby is not expecting that they will be playing very synchronous at the very first trial. She thinks that it may be André who adjusts his playing according to hers, as he has already listened to her. It seems that they are thinking the same thing. Interpreting the music the same way. Moving together in harmony. She has played this piece together with her friends several times in the past, but nothing was comparable to André.

Although André is a virtuoso pianist, he knows how to be a good secondo (the player who plays the second piano). He makes the primo (the player who plays the first piano) shine while playing as secondo. She has imagined playing a piano four-hand duet perfectly with someone, but she never imagined that person would be André.

Whenever their arms brush against each other, Gaby is a bit distracted. André's arms look so strong and very masculine with subtle hair. Gosh, what is she thinking? She tries to concentrate on the piece rather than on the secondo.

Then, they finish.

"I think that was good!" Gaby says.

"It was good in the beginning but it seemed that you lost focus a little bit in the middle. Am I correct?" André asks. Oh my God! Did he notice that she was admiring his arms?

"Oh yes. Is it obvious?"

"Yes. But that's normal. Let's try again."

They keep practicing again and again. Sometimes André asks to repeat only certain parts he is not satisfied with. Gaby also asks to repeat the part that she wants to be more confident at. Time flies by and they realize that it is already lunch time. They take a break.

"That was really good! I am very satisfied with our last trial," André comments.

"Me too! Thanks a lot for your guidance." André did give her some good feedback. Such as, play lighter in certain parts. Make sure your effort seems effortless. And try to show the audience that you think playing piano is easy. Don't let them know that you are actually trying hard.

"My pleasure."

Gaby is glad that they have had breakfast earlier. André was right, they need to eat because playing piano is physically tiring too. And now Gaby feels hungry again.

Gaby excuses herself to check her phone to see if there is any text from Raphael or Michelle. There is none. It's noon, and she is wondering where Raphael and Michelle are right now. She already told them she would be busy today for practice. But she still wants to make sure they can enjoy their time without her. This vacation was her idea after all. She calls Raphael's phone.

Apparently Raphael and Michelle are still in the hotel and want to sleep a bit more. It seems that they are still jet lagged, as it is still early morning in Singapore time.

"Your siblings?" André asks after she ends her conversation.

"Yes. They still want to sleep a bit more."

"I see. Shall we have lunch then?" André asks. Oh, she would love that!

"Sure, why not. Where?"

"Let's explore the harbour front. Let's get out of this room for a couple of hours," André suggests.

"Sounds perfect to me." Gaby smiles. André calls Guillaume to ask if he would like to join them, but Guillaume says he is going to meet some friends. So, it will be just the two of them.

After practicing together for about three hours, she starts to feel comfortable around André. He maintains formality but he smiles often too. Interacting with André face-to-face like this is very different than watching him from the audience seat. On the stage, he displayed a more serious and melancholic side of him. But now, Gaby can see some warmth as well.

They leave the suite together.

Chapter 11

Tuesday Afternoon
Auckland

They walk along the waterfront pier from Sofitel. Gaby enjoys the view and the beautiful atmosphere. It is summer in December in New Zealand.

"How do you feel now? I think you are ready to perform." André opens the conversation.

"Yeah, it is not as bad as I think. The piece itself only takes approximately three minutes."

"True."

They enter an Italian restaurant that seems very comfortable, and then they take a seat by the window so that they can enjoy the harbour view.

"Do you want to play another piece for the concert in Switzerland?" André asks. Gaby is speechless again. He has not even seen Gaby perform in New Zealand.

"Oh, well, are you sure?"

"Yes. But this time I was thinking you can do it solo. How about Chopin's Nocturne? You can choose any Nocturne you are comfortable with."

"What will the audience think though? They pay to see your performance only. Not me."

"That is okay. I will still play the entire repertoire in my program anyway. Think of your performance as a bonus performance. And I can announce that you are my student."

Gaby is very tempted. She also trusts André. If André says she can perform and she deserves to perform, then she believes that.

"Okay. I can play Nocturne in C-Sharp minor. Is that too beginner for your concert?" Gaby asks. It is her favourite Nocturne and it does not require very demanding technique like other Nocturnes. She can play some of the harder ones, but since this is a professional concert, she does not want to take risks by playing the harder ones.

"Nope. That's a very beautiful piece. One of my favourites too. The technique is not difficult at all but the interpretation can be tricky. So, I think by tomorrow we will be ready with The Entertainer and we can start on this." André says. Their pasta arrives and they start eating. Initially, they eat in silence. But then Gaby is curious about something.

"Can I ask you something?"

"Yes, of course."

"Do you do this to people often? Like giving an opportunity to any stranger who plays piano to perform at your concert?"

"No. You are the first one."

"What makes you suddenly want to do this?"

"Well. First is because I enjoyed your performance back in Singapore. If I enjoyed it, my audience will enjoy it too. Moreover, I feel like our style is very similar. You probably noticed that when we played The Entertainer. It is as if we can read each other's minds when we play piano. So I think there won't be a problem allowing you to play in my concerts."

Of course they have similar styles, Gaby has been listening to his playing from his albums, YouTube, Spotify, and Instagram throughout her life.

"Is that the only reason? I mean, why do I feel like you want to leave a legacy before you retire." Gaby hopes she did not cross the line. They have only known each other for three days. Well, she's known him for a long time, but he did not know her at all. Surprisingly, André laughs. This is the first time Gaby sees he is laughing.

"You are very honest. You dare to say what's on your mind. I like that." André drinks his water before replying, "That is somewhat true actually. See, you can read my mind again. Not only in piano but in real life too."

"Oh, is it true? You want to leave a legacy? Why are you retiring at such a young age? If you want to leave a legacy, why not open a music school while still performing?" Gaby takes a risk to dig further.

"Unfortunately, it's more complicated than that." André stops there. Gaby knows she cannot dig anymore.

"Anyway, if your performance goes well and you really enjoy it, can you promise me something?" André asks.

"What is that?"

"Get a Bachelor of Music degree. I will write a good recommendation. But no pressure at all. Wait until we finish our performances this Saturday and in Geneva. See if becoming a concert pianist is something you want to do. I think you really have great potential. I don't know why you are doing accounting instead of piano."

"Oh. I think I am too old to go back to university and earn a music degree. I am twenty-five years old. Do you know that?"

"It does not matter. You are never too old for school. I started my undergraduate degree in finance when I was twenty-three after I finished my master's in music."

Gaby is surprised. She never knew that. It was never written anywhere in any of his biographies on the Internet.

"Really? I never knew that."

"Yes, and I continued my master's degree in finance when I was twenty-seven and finished by the time I was twenty-eight years old."

"Why did you study finance?"

"That's another long story. To summarize, my parents passed away six years ago, and my dad left me his private equity firm. As a pianist, I didn't know anything about finance. So, I decided to enroll at McGill while performing at the same time."

"I am sorry about your parents, but that is very impressive. How do you manage your schedule as a pianist and an owner of a firm?"

"I am not the CEO or anything. I am just one of the board members who has the majority of the voting rights. I only attend the quarterly meetings and when there are votings required to make major decisions. But in order to vote, I need to know what I am voting for. That's why I studied finance. So I usually practice every day for four or five hours and then work in the evening. Luckily my finance work is not a nine-to-five thing."

"Which one do you enjoy more, piano or finance?"

"I enjoy both. Both piano and finance can make other people happier. With piano, you see more immediate results such as when people smile or cry after listening to your playing. With finance, whether it is managing their business, or buying their stocks, or helping them with the IPO, the goal is to make the clients less stressed. But since I am better at piano, I prefer piano to finance."

"I totally can relate. As an accountant, I am doing audits for our clients. When I am doing it, if I don't think that my work is going to make my client less stressed, it is a redundant job with long hours. Maybe that's why I have not been very satisfied with where I am now. I haven't been able to see an immediate result just like you and your audience."

"I still don't understand though. Why do you pursue an accounting career instead of piano?"

"Initially, I decided to pursue accounting because of job security. Accounting is the next thing I enjoy doing after piano."

"Do you think you will be satisfied doing accounting for the rest of your life and satisfied with playing piano as a hobby?"

Gaby thinks about André's question for a while. Will she be satisfied with the status quo?

"I have to think about it."

"Playing piano as a hobby is good. It is fun. But I find that performing in concerts gives you a target, makes you push yourself, gives you motivation to always maintain and improve your technique, and helps you practice your self-discipline. You learn a lot about yourself, your emotions, and other people. You can also learn all that when you are playing piano as a hobby, but I can guarantee that it will not be as intense as if you become a concert pianist."

They finish their food but none of them wants to end their discussion. They continue to share their thoughts about music and life.

Chapter 12

Wednesday Afternoon
Auckland

Gaby started practicing at André's suite at the same time as the day before. With practice, Gaby has become very comfortable playing The Entertainer duet with André. After they finished lunch yesterday, they practiced for another three hours. This morning they practiced The Entertainer again and Gaby started practicing the Nocturne for the concert in Geneva. When you play pieces that you are already comfortable with, the concert is not as scary as you think. Gaby feels better about this upcoming concert at Auckland Town Hall this Saturday.

Her new friendship with André is also something she is grateful for. He has an amazing personality. He is mature, wise, and at the same time sensitive and caring too. He is truly a great mentor. He always makes sure Gaby is comfortable when practicing. He knows how to give constructive feedback without being discouraging.

Despite being busy practicing, Gaby finally can spend time with Raphael and Michelle as well. Last night they enjoyed dinner at Orbit 360, which is located on the top of the Sky Tower. They ate dinner while enjoying the Auckland city view. André felt guilty to monopolize Gaby and made her unable to spend more time with her brother and sister. So, they agreed that she can take a break from practicing tomorrow on Thursday and spend the full day with Raphael and Michelle. Gaby really appreciates that. But at the same time she also enjoys spending time with André. After the concerts end, she doesn't know if they will spend time like this again. Gaby will go back to work in Toronto and André will go back to Montreal.

Yesterday, she invited André and Guillaume to join the dinner at the Sky Tower with Raphael and Michelle. But unfortunately, André was busy. He had to practice his repertoire for the concerts. Now Gaby is the one who feels guilty. She monopolized André's piano yesterday. The more André practices with her, the less time André practices for himself. But he is too kind to admit that. It seems that André will perform some other Etudes as well as Polonaises for this Saturday. And they are not easy pieces at all. André also said that Gaby should just think about herself and don't worry about him. Another positive trait of André: he is very selfless!

"I think we made good progress today. I really appreciate your hard work, Gaby," André says after they finish their morning practice session.

"My pleasure. Thank you for the opportunity."

"By the way, what are you going to wear for this Saturday? Have you decided yet?" André asks.

"Oh no! I completely forgot about that. I don't have any decent clothes for a concert right now, but I can go shopping tomorrow. Michelle will be able to help me."

"I was thinking, why don't we go shopping now? We can just grab a quick lunch and then go to Newmarket," André suggests. Gaby blushes. Shopping with André? Wow. She thinks that most men do not like shopping, do they?

"If you don't mind, I don't mind."

"Perfect. Let's go."

They park their car and walk into one of the upscale boutiques in Broadway Street in Newmarket. Gaby sees a lot of beautiful dresses.

"Good morning Sir and Ma'am. How can I help you today?" The shop assistant greets them.

"We need long dresses for a piano concert for her. She will be performing this Saturday."

"Oh I see. Please come with me."

They follow the shop assistant to where all the formal long dresses are displayed. They all look very expensive.

"Gabs, why don't you pick three of your most favourites and I pick three myself. Let's aim to buy at least three today."

"Three? I can wear the same dress for the concert here and the concert in Geneva. Why do we need three?"

"I prefer you wear different dresses for the concert. And I want you to at least have one spare dress just in case."

"Oh okay."

She finally picks three of her favourites: a blue dress with spaghetti straps, a green off-the-shoulder dress, and a pink one-shoulder dress. André picks a red strapless dress, a pink strapless dress, and a purple sleeveless dress.

The shop assistant brings all six dresses to the dressing room and Gaby follows her. She also helps Gaby with the dress. Gaby actually hesitates to show it to André. What if he does not like it? But as this is his concert, he will have to approve it. Gaby tries the red strapless dress.

"What do you think?" She asks André shyly.

André looks speechless for a few seconds. "It looks amazing on you. I really like this one. Let's try the others before deciding," André comments.

After trying all those six dresses, they both agree on two dresses, which are the blue dress with spaghetti straps and the pink strapless dress. For the third one, Gaby prefers the green dress while André prefers the red dress.

"The blue and pink dresses give a sweet and elegant impression. If someday you perform in cities like New York or Shanghai or Hong Kong, we need a glamorous impression. The red one gives that impression. What do you think?"

"I think the cut is too low. Don't you think so?" She suddenly feels embarrassed.

"Do you wear dresses often or go to parties often?"

"Not really."

"That's why. Trust me. It looks fine. But if you really like the green, we can buy it too."

"Oh no, that's okay. I picked the green one only because you said we need three. I am happy with the blue and the pink."

"Okay, let's pay."

They walk to the counter. Each of the three dresses costs more than a thousand New Zealand dollars. Gaby is shocked! But since this is for prestigious concerts, she thinks it's worth it to spend that much money. When she offers her credit card to the shop assistant, André quickly pushes that away.

"Don't be silly. I will pay."

"But why? I will be the one who will wear them."

"I am the one who asked you." Gaby cannot complain and she puts her credit card back in her wallet. Again, Gaby feels appreciated because André always asks for her opinion instead of deciding all by himself even though he has more experience. Even if there is disagreement between them, he considers her perspective too before making decision. The more she gets to know this man, the more she likes him

*

Wednesday Evening
Opera Suite, Sofitel

After dropping Gaby off at Pullman, André returns to his suite and starts practicing his other repertoire for the concert. They really had a great time today. Gaby looked really beautiful in all the dresses that she tried. The blue dress will be suitable for this Saturday and the pink dress will be suitable for the concert in Geneva. He is planning to get Gaby to perform in New York as well, but the concert in New York will be slightly different from the concerts in Singapore, Auckland, and Geneva. In New York, he will be playing Piano Concertos with the New York Philharmonic Orchestra. If he is bringing a guest performer, it will be ideal to put her almost at the end of the performance. André will find out how he can fit Gaby into his concert in New York. And if she is going to perform in New York, that red dress will be very suitable. She looks so alluring and glamorous in that dress. It gives the impression of a strong and capable woman. He cannot stop imagining her performing in that dress.

André's type is actually not an alluring and glamorous woman who wears a lot of makeup and dresses up with revealing clothes. His type of woman is actually a smart, sweet, and caring woman. He puts the same weight on both inner and outer beauty. But he cannot get rid of the image of Gaby looking very sexy in her dress. Gosh. What is he thinking? He does not want to ruin their new friendship with an unhealthy attraction that leads only to lust.

André tries to switch his focus back to his music. It is true that by involving Gaby, he has less time to practice by himself. But he notices that since he has been spending more time with Gaby, he is playing in a livelier and more expressive way. He is surprised by how much she influences him.

After he finishes practice, he walks to his room to grab his laptop. On the way to his room, he suddenly feels dizzy and a bit nauseous. He feels like the room is spinning until he has to lean against the wall to prevent him from falling. Guillaume arrives at just the right time.

"Oh my God, André, are you okay?" Guillaume grabs his shoulder while examining his face. André's face does not look good. It looks bloodless and pale. Guillaume is wondering how long he has been like this.

"I'm okay. Just tired. Too much practice." André closes his eyes with a hope that once he opens them the room will stop spinning.

"Let's get you to bed." André leans against Guillaume to get into the bedroom.

"Do you want me to call a doctor?" Guillaume asks while helping his friend lie down on the bed.

"No. I will be fine after getting some rest." Even though André is not sure about that. His breathing becomes irregular and his chest feels tight. 'Please not now. I still have three more concerts...'

Chapter 13

Thursday
Auckland

Today is a family day for Gaby. She will practice again tomorrow at Auckland Town Hall.

Gaby, Raphael, and Michelle spend the whole day exploring the city. In the morning, they walk along Queen Street to do some shopping and enjoy their bonding time in the coffee shop.

"So how's the preparation for the concert going?" Raphael asks.

"It's really good actually. I am ready for this Saturday and I am practicing a piece for next week in Geneva as well. It went really well. André is a really good teacher," Gaby explains. Raphael and Michelle were super excited and impressed when Gaby told them that she will be performing in Geneva as well.

"Nice. Glad to hear. And how's André himself?" Michelle asks.

"What about him?"

"You know what I am talking about," Michelle continues.

"You mean our relationship? I think I can say that we have become good friends right now. We have so many similarities and common interests. And he is being respectful all the time. He has good manners."

"Ah, everything always starts with being good friends first," Raphael comments.

"Well, I don't want to think about a relationship right now. What is more important is our upcoming concert." Gaby drinks her cappuccino.

"Oh right, it's true. I really cannot wait for Saturday! It's only two days away!" Raphael says.

"Yeah. Me too!"

After coffee, they continue their sightseeing. The transportation system in Auckland is not as good as in Singapore, so they take an Uber from place to place. Their next destination is Mt. Eden. It is a suburb area located in the southeast, only 15 minutes drive from downtown. From the top of the hill, they are able to enjoy the city view. And not only the city, but also the harbour, water, and some smaller islands across the main island. If she could describe the city as a color, it would be blue. She understands why Auckland is called the City of Sails.

After Mt. Eden, their next stop is Mission Bay, which is a beach located on the east side of the city. The beach is very beautiful and not too crowded on Thursday afternoon. They find a spot to sit on the sand. Gaby is enjoying her time looking at the horizon and the blue water. There are birds flying and chirping as well. She finds that New Zealand is similar to Canada. It is a multicultural and peaceful country.

Their last stop for the day is the Ponsonby area. They enjoy dinner and drink at a bar with live music. Gaby does not want to drink too much as she has to practice tomorrow. They end up spending time chatting and dancing with people from other groups. They are mostly local people from Auckland. Raphael ends up a bit drunk and dances with a pretty kiwi girl. Michelle gets into a long conversation with a cute blonde guy. There is this cute guy too who tries to initiate a conversation with Gaby.

"Oh you are from Canada? Cool. I like your accent," the guy says in kiwi accent.

"Thank you."

"So what brings you to New Zealand?"

"Oh, I am here to watch a concert."

"What concert?"

"A piano concert. Do you know André Gauthier-Lee?"

"Yes I do! Even though I don't play piano that much, I know him from YouTube. He is very good and very famous here, too. But wait, isn't he from Canada?"

"Yes he is."

"Then why don't you watch him in Canada? Why come all the way here?"

Gaby only smiles. She starts imagining André's face. She realizes that she misses him. She misses playing piano with him, talking with him, and spending time with him.

*

Thursday
Sofitel

André feels better today. After sleeping longer hours than usual, he is ready to practice piano and catch up with work. The repertoire in Auckland is as challenging as the repertoire in Singapore, however the pieces will be shorter, unlike the four Chopin's Ballades he played in Singapore. So he can be a bit more relaxed this time.

Without Gaby, his suite feels emptier. Hopefully Guillaume will be back soon. André finishes practicing early and then reviews new reports for Gauthier Capital. The share price for the IPO seems a bit too low in his opinion. He is trying to review the facts and the numbers again.

Guillaume enters the suite. He brings some dinner, which is a Korean Bulgogi. André cannot thank him more. He does not realize that it's six already.

"Are you feeling better today?" Guillaume asks.

"Yes, much better. Thanks for asking and thanks for the dinner."

"Are you sure you don't need to see a doctor or anything?"

"No, I am fine."

"Alright." They eat dinner in silence.

"How's Gaby? Is she ready for Saturday?" Guillaume asks.

"Yes. She is more than ready. She works hard."

"Glad to hear. And you seem happier and more relaxed when she is around. Is something going on between you two?"

André laughs. "Am I? She is fun to be around. Smart and brave as well. But right now, we will focus on the concert before anything else."

"Ah, I see. Can her presence change your mind about..." Guillaume does not finish his sentence but André knows what he is talking about.

"It's still too early to decide but I might want to continue fighting until the end."

"I see. I can see that she is special."

"She is."

André realizes that he misses her already. He misses playing piano with her, talking to her, and spending time with her.

*

Friday Afternoon
Auckland Town Hall

Gaby has just arrived at Auckland Town Hall for the final rehearsal. Guillaume picked her up at Pullman this afternoon and they drove together. Guillaume said that André has arrived for the rehearsal an hour before her and he has already been practicing by himself. Today is important because she will be practicing on the same piano as the concert day.

The Great Hall itself is impressive. It is huge with a high ceiling and it has three levels. The capacity is about fifteen hundred. There is also a giant organ behind the stage.

Gaby sits in the front row with Guillaume, enjoying André's performance. He is currently playing Grande Valse Brillante Op. 18. André is only wearing a white polo shirt and jeans. But he looks so good in everything he wears. She feels like she is watching a private concert. It is only her and Guillaume in the audience seats. André plays every piece twice and he never makes mistakes. Gaby is impressed. Now, André is playing his last piece before the duet.

"Gaby, are you ready? After this it's your turn right?" Guillaume asks.

"Yes." Gaby answers. Her hands turn cold.

"You will be great!"

"Thank you!"

When André finishes his piece, Gaby walks on the stage towards him and towards the piano. André is already standing beside the piano. He smiles at her. Now Gaby is facing the high ceiling hall, the empty audience seats in the main floor as well as in the balconies. Gaby feels like she can be swallowed by the great hall. Most of the time she is in the audience. But this time she is on stage!

"Ready?" André asks.

"Yes."

They bow towards the empty red audience seats, pretending that there are real people there even though Guillaume is the only person who sits there. Guillaume gives them applause and they grab a seat on the piano bench. She takes the seat on the right side which is closer to the audience, while André sits on the left. Then, they play together in harmony.

The piano on stage is slightly heavier than the baby grand piano at André's suite. It's good that she gets a chance to try it before the actual concert. She adjusts her touch quickly. They play four times in a row. Thankfully they make no mistakes. This increases Gaby's confidence for tomorrow.

When they finish, they bow again to the empty audience seats. The piece they have just played together is the last piece.

"Well done, Gabs. I think you are ready," André says.

"Thanks. Your practice session was also as awesome as usual."

"Thank you. Would you mind giving me another fifteen minutes? I want to practice some pieces one more time. And then you can practice again if you want."

"Sure, no rush." Gaby walks down the stage and sits beside Guillaume.

"Well done, Gabs." Guillaume comments.

"Thank you."

"By the way, do you notice that André's performances are a bit different now?" Guillaume asks.

"Different in what way?"

"Like, livelier and more colorful, I presume."

Gaby turns her eyes to André on the stage. He is playing Etude in F Major Op. 10 No. 8 (Sunshine). After twenty years of listening to his music, Gaby agrees with Guillaume. André plays it more energetically and in a livelier and more colourful way.

Chapter 14

Saturday Evening
Auckland Town Hall

For the whole first session, Gaby is sitting in the audience seat on the main floor. She can see André's skillful hands as well as his expression. Gaby reads the full list of the repertoire for today:

Chopin - Etude in G-flat Major Op. 10 No. 5 (Black Keys)

Chopin - Etude in F Major Op. 10 No. 8 (Sunshine)

Chopin - Grande Valse Brillante in E-flat Major Op. 18

Chopin - Scherzo in B-flat minor Op. 31

Chopin - Polonaise in A Major Op. 40 No. 1 (Military)

˜Intermezzo˜

Chopin - Etude in A minor Op. 10 No. 2 (Chromatic)

Chopin - Etude in G-flat Major Op. 25 No. 9 (Butterfly)

Chopin - Polonaise in A-flat Major Op. 53 (Heroic)

Joplin - The Entertainer

Even though she listened to his repertoire yesterday, she is still impressed today. The mood for today's concert is different from the mood in Singapore's concert. In Singapore, the aura was strong, thrilling, and lonely. Today the aura is energetic, lively, and humorous. André looks really cool on the stage. This time he looks very professional in his white shirt, bow tie, and black suit jacket. His hair is slicked back as usual. It still feels like a dream that she has spent hours upon hours practicing, having lunch, and shopping with this man who is currently sitting behind the piano and playing in a very sophisticated way. Gaby cannot believe that she will join him there soon, even though it is only for one piece.

During the intermezzo, Gaby, Michelle, and Raphael go into the green room. Michelle will help Gaby get changed and re-touch her make-up if necessary. Raphael is following them because he is "curious" about what the backstage looks like.

When they enter the green room, André and Guillaume are already there. André and Guillaume seem to be surprised to see her.

"Wow Gaby, you look so different. You are very beautiful," André comments. Whenever she was with him, she barely applied any make up. Today, Michelle has styled Gaby's hair for an up do style. Then she applied fake eyelashes and blush as well. Gaby looks very different than her usual self. She looks more mature and very beautiful.

"Thank you. Your performance during the first session went really well. You seem to be happier today too," Gaby comments.

"I am." André smiles at her.

André and Guillaume introduce themselves and shake hands with Raphael and Michelle. Michelle asks Raphael to take a picture of her and André. Even Raphael wants to take a picture with André as well! Gaby has just realized that she herself has not taken any picture with André! Even though she is the one who is a big fan of him, and there were tons of opportunities when they practiced together or spent time together. How could she forget?

Then, André, Guillaume, and Raphael leave Gaby and Michelle in the room to get changed. Gaby will be wearing her blue dress with spaghetti straps. When she is done, André, Guillaume, and Raphael re-enter the room.

"Oh my God, is this even my sister? You look stunning!" Raphael comments. Now with the make-up, hair, and dress, Gaby looks like a professional pianist.

"Thank you, Raphael," Gaby says. She glances towards André. André seems speechless as well. For some reason Gaby smiles to herself. And then they hear an announcement that session two will begin soon. Guillaume, Raphael, and Michelle wish her good luck and return to the great hall. Now it is only André and her in the green room.

"How are you feeling?" André asks.

"Nervous. The audience is full. And they all seem to be classical music admirers."

"That's even better. Don't worry. You are ready. I have faith in you. When you are on the stage, don't think about the audience. Focus on listening to your music only."

"Yes. I will keep that in mind. Thank you. And by the way, you played really well in the first session. Keep it up!"

"Thank you!" André leaves to go back to the stage.

During session two, Gaby will be listening from the backstage until it is her turn to perform. This is the most nerve-wracking experience. Waiting for your turn to perform. She is waiting there for about an hour and then André finishes his last piece, which is the Polonaise Heroic, before their piece. Her heart beats so hard and fast. 'Gaby, calm down,' she says to herself. She keeps repeating what André told her. Don't think about the audience. Think about the music. Then, she hears André make an announcement.

"Ladies and Gentlemen, may I introduce you to my new student from Canada, Gabrielle Zhang. She and I will be playing a special repertoire. Let's give her a big round of applause!"

Gaby hears a loud applause and she walks towards the stage. When she enters the stage, the spotlight focuses on her. She stands beside André, and then André grabs her hand and they bow together. André's hand is as cold as hers. Is he nervous too? That does not show at all. Luckily, the lights are dimmed so she cannot see the faces in the audience.

She takes a seat and they start playing. It feels like they were back in his suite when they were the only people in the room, playing together. She focuses on her music. They share a light and humorous feeling with the audience, as this is how they interpret the piece.

In the middle of the performance, someone from the audience shouts something Gaby could not hear clearly. As she follows what André said, Gaby keeps playing her piece as though nothing happened. She does not realize what is happening. Then, there is another shout from the same person. The spectators seem to be distracted and whisper to one another. When Gaby starts to notice, the piece is almost done. Why is the audience whispering? Gaby keeps going. She has to finish the piece no matter what happens. Being on stage does not feel real to her. She shuts out all her senses other than listening to the sound of her own music.

And then, they finish the piece perfectly.

Gaby freezes for a while. What happened? André rises from his seat and offers his hand. He smiles at Gaby and nods. Gaby takes his hand and then rises. They bow to the audience. Only half of the audience gives them sincere applause. The remaining half is still whispering.

Then, Gaby and André walk towards the backstage. After they leave the stage, Gaby realizes what the spectator was shouting:

Amateur! Get off the stage!

*

Gaby is in the green room with André. André is still holding her hands. Gaby is still shocked about what has happened.

"Gaby, listen to me, that was so awesome! I am very proud of you. Trust me. Don't think about anything else," André says. He puts his hands on Gaby's shoulders.

"But what has just happened? Did I ruin the performance? Did they say amateur?" Gaby feels like someone stabs her in the chest. It hurts so much.

"Don't worry. I will handle that. It was just someone who was jealous of your performance. Okay? I will be back soon, wait for me here. Okay?"

Gaby nods. André lets go of her hands. She feels lonely and cold in that room. At some point during her practice sessions in André's suite, she thought that this opportunity could be a turning point in her life. She could finally call herself a musician, and not just a CPA. She wanted to be someone who can share the music with the audience too. But after tonight, she is not sure anymore. Her confidence has shattered. Maybe she just doesn't have what it takes to be a pianist. Before she can think of anything else, there is a knock on the door and then Guillaume, Raphael, and Michelle enter the room.

"Gabs! You are so awesome! I am so proud of you!" Raphael and Michelle hug her tightly. Gaby releases herself. "What happened? Am I like an amateur? Why did they say that?"

"No, Gaby. Don't listen to them. Please. It's just one crazy spectator. You were awesome out there," Guillaume says.

Then Gaby hears André play one more piece. He is playing Fantaisie Impromptu Op. 66. The bright mood that he displayed since the beginning of the concert changes. He plays this piece like he is protesting against the audience and is agitated. After he finishes, the audience gives him a big round of applause. It is definitely more applause than when they performed together. Gaby decides to sit. She has no more energy to stand. Everything seems wrong. Being here is wrong. She starts to believe that she looks like an amateur and does not deserve to be here. She just does not want to talk to anyone.

Then André comes back to the green room. He looks so handsome and sophisticated. Unlike her. What on earth was she thinking to agree to be on stage with him? They are so different. She is just ruining his concert. He quickly walks towards her and grabs her hands. Gaby feels like she wants to throw up.

"Gaby, how do you feel right now?" André lowers himself to his knees in front of her. He looks at her in the eyes. "Do you trust me when I said that you were awesome out there? I am very happy to perform with you!"

"No. I just ruined your performance. They know that I am an amateur." Gaby tries not to cry. She does not want to have drama in her life. She tries to act cool like nothing has happened. Deep down she feels hurt and embarrassed. But she does not want to show it to anyone. Not to André and Guillaume. Not even to Raphael and Michelle.

"That is not true. Why are you letting a crazy spectator's comments ruin your confidence? Why do you believe her more than you believe me?"

"You are just trying to make me feel better."

"No, I am not. I am telling you the truth," André replies. Gaby does not know what to say.

"We need to talk, Gaby. But not here." André turns to Michelle, "Can you please help Gaby get changed? Then we can talk at my place, okay?" Michelle nods. André, Guillaume, and Raphael leave them for a while.

"Michelle, I am doomed. What was I thinking?" Gaby asks her sister when they are alone in the room.

"No, you are not. She was just one crazy spectator. The security officers have dealt with her. She was just jealous of you because you are very talented and stunning and you won André's heart."

"But the audience barely gave applause for our performance. It wasn't that I was expecting big applause or anything, but even if the pianist plays really badly, the audience usually still gives applause for courtesy right? What am I doing wrong?"

"It is because they were still shocked with that stupid girl who shouted by the time you and André finished playing. They were not sure how to react."

"And then André had to go back to give a better closing performance to fix the situation."

"Gabs, c'mon. Don't beat yourself up like this. Let's go. Let's leave this place."

Michelle grabs all her stuff and they walk out. André, Guillaume, and Raphael seem to be talking with two security officers and two ushers. André leaves the conversation as soon as he sees Gaby.

"Gabs, I am gonna get changed and then we'll talk, okay?" André taps her shoulder to give assurance. She nods.

After André has changed, they leave the town hall through the back door so that they don't have to bump into the audience. They wait outside the door when Guillaume gets the car. Finally the car appears and they go inside the car.

Since they left the green room, André never let go of her hands.

Chapter 15

Saturday Evening
Sofitel

Gaby is sitting in André's bed in his Opera Suite with Raphael and Michelle. Raphael and Michelle cannot stop saying how amazing her performance was. Gaby is just listening to them without making any comments. She just nods and says okay to whatever they say to her. She knows that they are trying to make her feel better. But nothing can make her feel better. She just feels tired and she wants to forget everything.

André appears in the doorway carrying a mug. He sits on the edge of the bed. "Here, drink this. It's hot chocolate. Hopefully it can make you sleep better tonight." André gives the mug to Gaby. Gaby receives it. "Thank you."

Then Raphael and Michelle excuse themselves as it is obvious that André needs to talk to Gaby privately. They close the door to give André and Gaby some privacy.

"Gabs, I know that whatever I say will not make you feel better. If I were in your position, I would handle it the same way as you did."

Gaby only smiles and drinks her hot chocolate.

"What impressed me was that you kept playing and you didn't stop until you finished. Other people in your position would have given up, but you didn't. You handled yourself very well. You pretended nothing happened. You bowed to the audience." André stops for a second. "That is how a true professional would react."

"Thanks. I was just following your advice. Focus on listening to my music only. So I did not realize what had happened until I left the stage.

It's not about professionalism. I just did not hear it or think about it clearly when I was on stage."

"Please Gabs, don't let the audience affect you. We have played our music beautifully and perfectly. There was nothing else we could have done better. Am I right?"

"You probably could have done better by not inviting me to the stage to perform with you. We should have expected something like this."

"I don't regret my decision even for a second. This is one of the best decisions I have made throughout my entire career."

"But this event will be talked about. They will never think of you the same way as before."

"That is exactly what I want. I'll leave a legacy by training someone to become a professional pianist too," André says. Gaby doesn't know what to say.

"Gaby, I don't want you to say anything else today. But I think I should let you know what's in my mind right now. I am very satisfied with our duet today. And I want to stick to our original plan. You are going to perform your solo in Geneva. Also, after seeing your performance tonight, I will have you perform with me in New York too."

*

Sunday Morning
Sofitel

Gaby opens her eyes. For a second, she forgets where she is. She sees sunlight coming through the window. Then she is aware of where she is. She is in André's bedroom.

She thought she was not going to be able to sleep well after what happened last night. Surprisingly, she slept very well and that was thanks to a beautiful melody coming from the living room. André must have been playing that to help her sleep.

She wakes up from the bed and walks into the bathroom. She sees herself in the mirror. She is wearing her pajamas and her plain face stares back at her from the mirror. After they left the town hall last night, they stopped by Pullman first because Michelle had to pack Gaby's stuff as André wanted Gaby to stay with him at Sofitel. She was grateful to Michelle. And then Michelle also helped her clean up the makeup from her face last night. A disappointment comes across Gaby's chest again. André and Michelle have put so much effort into making her presentable on stage, but it did not work out so well. How would André and Michelle feel? Do they feel that all their efforts were useless?

Suddenly she hears a knock on the door. She opens the door and sees André standing there. His hair is everywhere but he still looks good. It seems that he has also just woken up. He wears a white shirt and khaki shorts.

"Good morning, Gaby. Did you sleep well?" André asks.

"Yes. Thanks. Maybe I should get going now."

"Oh, relax. I want to take you to the beach today. Are you interested?"

Today is Sunday. It is her last day in Auckland. Tomorrow morning she will fly to Geneva. But how about André? Isn't he supposed to leave this afternoon?

André seems to be able to read her mind. "I changed my flight to tomorrow morning too."

"Why? It's not because of me, is it?"

"I just want to spend more time in Auckland with you."

"Alright. What time do you want to go?"

"Get ready, and pack your swimsuit. Then, join me at the dining table for breakfast. We'll go after that."

"Okay. Sounds good. Give me fifteen minutes."

"No rush."

Chapter 16

Sunday Afternoon
Piha Beach

Gaby didn't expect that André would take her as far as Piha Beach. Piha beach is a one-hour drive from downtown Auckland. It is a very beautiful beach located in the Waitakere Range Regional Parks. Unlike Mission Bay where you still can feel that you are in the city, Piha beach is a real beach overlooking the Tasman Sea directly.

Along the drive from downtown to Piha Beach, they did not talk much. Gaby enjoyed the ride and lost herself in her own thoughts. André also seemed to be busy in his own thoughts. Gaby was glad that André did not push her to talk either. They enjoyed the silence and they didn't need to fill the silence with a talk. For them, silence is not something awkward, it is a time to reflect and to be more aware of your surroundings.

The sky turns grey just as they arrive. It is a sign that it is probably going to rain soon. Gaby does not feel like swimming.

"I think I will walk along the shore instead of swimming. But you can go ahead," she says to André.

"I don't feel like swimming either. Let's just walk."

They start walking towards the beach. They are the only people on the beach today. It's a bit strange considering that it is Sunday. They walk in silence for about fifteen minutes. Gaby feels the breeze and enjoying the wave sounds. She starts to feel better.

"André, I just want to say thank you for everything. I know you tried to cheer me up and make me feel better after what happened last night. I really appreciate your support." Gaby opens the conversation. She has a lot to thank André for.

"Don't worry. It was also my fault. If I didn't insist on you performing with me, you probably wouldn't feel like this right now. You would probably be having fun with Raphael and Michelle, instead of stuck with me for hours practicing," André says. He is looking at his feet instead of looking at Gaby.

"Please, don't let my mood affect you. You are still happy with our performance last night right?"

"Yes. I absolutely am. But I feel like I am being too ambitious and end up pushing you too hard to fulfil my ambition. If you want to blame someone for what has happened, blame me."

Gaby chuckles. "How can I blame you? I know you mean well. This has nothing to do with you. This is just my insecurity. I haven't performed internationally like this before. I have not been performing for a while. This makes me feel insecure, as I have not had any history of success with something like this. When the audience gave bad feedback, it affected me too much because I still relied on validation from them."

"Can validation from me be enough?"

"I am working on believing it."

"Let me show you something." André takes out his phone from his shorts' pocket. He scrolls through his phone until he finds something. "Here look at these. These are some of my fans messaging me about how great your performance was."

André shows her some comments after last night's performance. Gaby reads some comments that say:

Gabrielle played amazingly! You guys were very in sync with each other!

Your student is stunning. She is gorgeous and she played very well.

Why hasn't she performed that much if she is that good?

Which music school does she attend?

"Do you believe me now?" André puts back his phone to his pocket.

"Thanks for showing me that. I still think that if I am that good, no spectator would complain like the one who shouted at me."

"That's silly. I have more than a thousand people who dislike my YouTube posts. No matter how good you are, you have to accept that there will always be some people who don't appreciate your work and disagree with your interpretation and so on."

"I guess you are right."

"I am very happy that we were able to perform together," André continues.

"Me too, despite what happened. Do you know that I have been listening to you since I was five years old? I know that this is embarrassing. But you are my idol. I always wanted to be as good as you. When I took piano lessons, whenever I felt that it was too hard and challenging, I would go back and listen to your album. That was like a remedy. I became motivated again every time I listened to you playing. You are such an inspiration." Gaby confesses.

André seems surprised by her compliment. "Wow, thank you for thinking that highly of me. I appreciate your honesty. It makes me feel good knowing that I am indirectly motivating people to keep playing piano and not giving up."

"Yes, and whenever you came to perform in Toronto, I never missed it. When I heard that you are retiring, and you are giving your last concerts, I planned this trip right away. So, you can imagine how I felt when you asked me to perform with you."

"Yes. Like it's unreal."

"Exactly. It's like my dream came true. If I am dreaming, I don't want to wake up."

"So imagine this, what happened last night was only a brief nightmare in your dream. But your dream has not finished. Don't you want your dream to have a happy ending?"

"Yes I do want that. But I am not sure if I still have the opportunity."

"What are you talking about? Of course you do. Please perform again in Geneva and in New York."

"What if what happened last night happens again? It will affect you too. These are your last concerts."

"If it happens again, it happens. I don't care how it affects me. I only care if it affects you or if it hurts you. But if I only think about myself, I honestly don't care about what the audience thinks anymore. I am very satisfied with what we have come up with so far and that is enough for me."

Gaby does not know what to say. They look at each other in the eyes. Gaby can see sincerity in his words. André truly believes in what he is doing. And once he is determined, he will not let anyone ruin his vision.

Gaby is really touched by André's kindness. He cares about her feelings. He is protective and gentle. Gaby cannot hold her tears anymore.

"Oh, no Gaby, I am so sorry. I don't mean to hurt you."

"No, I am crying not because I am hurt or anything. It's just you have been very kind to me." Gaby looks at the ground. She hates crying in front of people.

"And last night, were you playing those pieces to help me sleep? It was definitely very helpful. If I couldn't sleep, I would be busy thinking about negative things. Replaying what had happened and so on. But thanks to you, I fell asleep faster. You always give more than what is expected. For your mentorship and support, I cannot thank you enough."

André cannot hold himself back anymore. He steps forward and hugs her tight. He puts his arms around her. Her head is against his chest. Gaby can hear André's heartbeat. It beats very fast. She can feel his breathing too. André does not want to let Gaby go. He wants to stop the time and hold her forever.

They don't know how long they are hugging. They release each other only when it starts raining. "Let's go back?" André says with a smile.

"Let's go," Gaby says. She feels much better after talking heart to heart with André like this. They walk back to the car but now they both are soaking wet in the rain. André's white shirt clings tightly to his skin, showing a well-defined physique underneath the shirt. Gaby tries to look elsewhere.

"Well, at least we have spare clothes. I will let you get changed inside the car. Let me know when you are done."

"Okay." Gaby reaches her bag from the back seat and grabs a shirt. She changes quickly and hangs the wet shirt to the grab handle on the back. She knocks the car window where André is leaning back against. He gets inside the car.

"I will have to change too." André is pointing at his wet shirt. He starts unbuttoning his shirt while grabbing his dry shirt from his bag on the back seat. He frees himself from his wet shirt, showing his lean and toned body. He even has a six-pack! Why is he so perfect in everything?

Gaby quickly turns her head and looks ahead instead of looking at him. She doesn't want to be caught staring at his perfect body. André finishes buttoning his shirt and starts driving.

"Do you want to have some hot drinks?"

"Yes, I would love to."

"Okay, we can go to Devonport and enjoy the nice view and the rain."

"Sounds perfect." Gaby smiles. Her mood seems to be brighter.

*

Sunday Evening
Devonport

The drive from Piha Beach to Devonport has been quiet and relaxing. André plays Chopin's Ballades in the car. Gaby enjoys the ride in silence. Gaby likes that both of them are comfortable with each other so they don't need to fill in the silence with a conversation.

Today is their last day in Auckland. Gaby wants to enjoy the view. They pass Auckland Harbour Bridge on the way to Devonport. They can see downtown Auckland from the other side of the bay. André keeps driving along the highway and then they pass some suburban areas and they arrive at Devonport. Devonport is a suburban area in the North Shore. There is also a ferry port from downtown that goes straight to Devonport. As it is too early to have dinner, they grab coffee and walk along Victoria Road that ends up in the pier. Luckily, the rain has stopped.

"André, have you ever felt that you are not good enough as a pianist?" Gaby asks as they enjoy the downtown view from the pier. She has wanted to interview him for a long time. Gaby is very curious.

"Oh yes, of course. I think everybody does."

"How come? You are very confident on the stage, and always play perfectly."

"In terms of technique, maybe yes. But playing piano is more than just technique. There had been times when my piano teacher said that I played like a robot. Especially in the beginning of my career when I was still young. Also, I have had people throw nasty comments at me on social media. There are a few composers that I am still having a hard time interpreting. There were times when I reached out to some orchestras and venues around the world, but I only got rejected or ignored."

"Oh, I never imagined that someone like you had also gone through that process. I thought all the orchestras and venues around the world were the ones who invited you?"

"Well, in most cases yes, but not always. Every time I won a prestigious competition, I was sought after. Or after I delivered an outstanding performance with a prestigious orchestra or in a prestigious venue, then yes. But there was some downtime too. It is up and down and is not steady. So, if you want to be a concert pianist for a living, you have to be ready to see fluctuations in your income."

"I see. What else are the challenges of being a concert pianist?"

"Being a concert pianist also requires physical strength and good stamina. The travels can make you prone to sickness. There were times when I was very sick but I still had to perform and practice because I couldn't cancel the performance. Also, there were times when I had to play with an orchestra, but I didn't enjoy the piece. And I still had to practice hard for that piece. The travel is also very tiring. It was fun in the beginning, but over time, you get burned out and you just want to settle down. Right now, you are experiencing it for yourself. Imagine if you were doing this throughout your life."

Gaby thinks about André's words. It makes sense. Gaby always thought that André's world was perfect. Now, Gaby feels more sympathetic towards him. He has shown her his vulnerability too.

"It's a lonely job too. Because I constantly travel, I don't have much time to spend with friends. I don't have any family other than Guillaume. I think you are very lucky to have Raphael and Michelle."

"Yes I think I am."

"Both of your parents live in Toronto as well?"

"Yes, they do."

"If you don't mind me asking, do you have a Chinese descent?"

"No, I don't mind at all. My parents were born in Hong Kong. They immigrated to Canada when they were teenagers. But Raphael, Michelle, and I were born in Toronto."

"I see. My mother was from South Korea. She immigrated to Canada when she was a teenager. My father was *Québécois*. So, I have a mixed blood."

"I know. It is written on Wikipedia," Gaby says with a smile. André laughs at her comment.

"It was hard for me when they passed away. That was the lowest point in my life. I was just two months away from graduation. They had booked their tickets to Paris and I had imagined that they would attend my graduation, watch me perform, and we would go skiing in the Alps together. But it did not happen."

"I am sorry."

"That's okay. I actually did not want to come back to Montreal. There were too many memories of my parents. But my dad left me the firm. So it was better for me to settle in Montreal."

"At least you still have Guillaume. And now you have me, Raphael, and Michelle. We all can be friends even after this concert tour is finished."

André does not reply. He does not know what to say. He would love to continue the friendship with Gaby. He would like for them to be even more than just friends... He does not know if she is single or not. He likes her and he feels comfortable opening up to her even though they have only known each other for a week. He feels like he has known her for ages. André appreciates Gaby's honesty when she admitted that she is his fan. He does not think less of Gaby because she is his fan. In fact, he feels honored.

They continue their deep conversation during a dinner at Devon on the Wharf. It is a restaurant on the pier where they can enjoy the harbour view and downtown view from afar. This time they see the Auckland night lights. The lights are so pretty. Gaby will never be bored with this kind of view. Tonight is more special because it is with André.

At ten, they drive back to downtown. They pass Auckland Harbour Bridge again, but this time they enjoy the night view while listening to Chopin's Nocturnes. Half an hour later they enter the downtown area.

Gaby decides that she will stay at Pullman with Raphael and Michelle as they must be worried about her after what happened last night. They stop at Sofitel to get Gaby's stuff and then André drives her back to Pullman.

"Thank you very much for today, André. I feel like I am very burdensome," Gaby says when André pulls his car in front of the lobby to drop her off.

"Not at all. So, are you still going to perform in Geneva and New York? You haven't given me an answer."

It takes Gaby almost a minute to think. If she quits now, the last concert would be a bad memory. But if she is willing to take risks and try again, she has an opportunity to create a better memory.

"Count me in," Gaby answers. André looks pleased.

"Really? Thank you so much Gaby! I knew you wouldn't give up. You are very strong."

Chapter 17

Monday Morning
Auckland International Airport

Gaby, Raphael and Michelle arrive at Auckland International Airport two hours before their departure. They are waiting for André and Guillaume to check in together. André has advised them that they will be flying together to Geneva via Tokyo and London. It will be a long flight.

After arriving at Pullman yesterday, Gaby was not feeling well. During the night, she ran a fever. André was right: travelling too much can make you prone to sickness. Only half way through the tour and Gaby is already down with fever. She feels chills, fatigue and headache. Raphael checked up on her this morning and gave her a Tylenol to temporarily reduce the fever.

"Let me know if you feel better. Otherwise, we can just extend our stay in Auckland until you do," Raphael says.

"No. I will have to perform in Geneva. I cannot stay here," Gaby insists.

"But you are not feeling well. And this is such a long flight. More than thirty hours. You will just get worse. I will have to tell André that you are unable to perform if you are not better by Saturday."

"No. Don't tell him, please. I am fine."

Raphael only sighs impatiently. He is very proud that his sister is able to perform on stage, but if these performances make her stressed, he would prefer that she just enjoy watching the concert. They are supposed to be on vacation.

Then, André and Guillaume appear. André looks very cool with sunglasses and a dark brown V-neck sweater, with a white shirt underneath and jeans. It is winter in Geneva, so all of them are ready in their warm clothes. Guillaume also wears sunglasses and a halter neck sweater with jeans. They both look like Hugo Boss models.

"Hi. How are you guys doing?"

"Good, thanks. You?" Gaby asks, as Raphael sighs.

"Good, thanks." André takes off his sunglasses and looks at Gaby. He notices that she is a bit pale and looks unwell.

"Gaby, what's wrong? Are you not feeling well?"

"I am good. Don't worry," Gaby says.

"She has had a fever since last night. Her temperature is thirty nine degrees," Raphael says to André.

André looks very worried. "Oh, no. Do you still want to fly today? We can postpone it until you feel better."

"No, please don't. I am fine. I want to leave for Geneva today."

"Are you guys flying in economy class?" André asks.

"Yes," Gaby answers.

"Let's have your seats upgraded. You will feel uncomfortable flying in economy class to Geneva in this condition."

"That is not necessary..." Gaby starts to protest, but André and Guillaume start walking to the check-in counter. Gaby, Raphael, and Michelle share a look. Is this for real?

André feels extremely guilty. Is Gaby sick because of him? Because he pushed her too much?

Their plane is taking off. Guillaume has successfully upgraded the seat for Raphael, Michelle, and Gaby. Unfortunately, due to the last minute upgrade, they cannot sit next to each other. André gives up his seat and Guillaume's for Gaby and Raphael to sit next to each other. André is sitting three rows behind, with Guillaume another two rows behind and Michelle one row behind Guillaume on the other side of the plane.

André releases his seatbelt and walks towards Raphael and Gaby's seats. Gaby is already asleep. She must feel very tired. He should not have taken her out yesterday. He regrets it. André drops to his knees so that he is at equal height with Gaby who is sleeping. He puts his hand on Gaby's forehead. Her fever does not seem too bad now, but it still feels warm.

"Is she getting better?" André asks Raphael.

"Only temporarily. I gave her Tylenol this morning."

"Okay. It is my fault that she got sick. I am so sorry."

"That's okay. She is so eager to perform with you. But if she does not get better by the time we arrive in Geneva, I will ask her to rest instead of practicing. Do you mind?"

"No, not at all. I absolutely agree. Her health is more important than practicing or performing. Please take care of her. Thank you Raphael." André rises to his feet.

Chapter 18

Tuesday Evening
Geneva

By the time their plane lands at Geneva, Gaby feels so much better. Gaby is very thankful that André has upgraded their seats to business class. She could not imagine sitting in economy for more than thirty hours. Also, when they laid over in Tokyo and London, they could wait for the next flight in the business lounge. The comfort speeds up Gaby's recovery.

André also canceled their reservation at the Tiffany Hotel. Instead, Gaby, Raphael, and Michelle will stay at Guillaume's suite at Beau Rivage. Initially, André and Guillaume booked connecting Lake View Loft Suites. But instead, Guillaume will stay with André.

That night, Gaby falls asleep right away. She hopes that tomorrow she will feel normal again and can start practicing for their next concert.

It is two in the morning and André is still catching up with work. He is working while enjoying a glass of scotch. He feels extremely tired after a thirty-hour flight, but this report needs to be reviewed. If this IPO is successful, it will mean a huge profit for the firm.

When he finishes his scotch, he goes downstairs to refill his glass. He finds that Guillaume is not sleeping yet. Guillaume is also enjoying a scotch while enjoying the view from the window. Even though it is dark outside, he can still see some lights surrounding Lake Leman.

"You aren't sleeping yet?" André asks.

"No. What about you?"

"Still need to catch up with work." André replies. "Are you sure you don't want to sleep in the bed? I don't mind sleeping on the couch."

"I am fine with the couch too," Guillaume says. André joins Guillaume in enjoying the view.

"Thanks for letting them use your suite."

"No problem. It is more convenient for Gaby and for you."

"True."

"How are you feeling? It's getting worse, isn't it?" Guillaume asks. He is still facing the window.

"It is. I am going to get a check-up though, right after the concert in New York."

"If everything works out well, are you going to continue to perform?"

"I'll probably take a year off. Assuming everything goes well," André replies. "Have you found another client yet?"

"No. I don't want to think about a new client while I am still with you."

"Thanks for always being by my side, Guillaume. Your support means a lot."

"Just try your best, André."

"I will."

*

Wednesday Morning
Beau Rivage

That morning, the five of them are enjoying breakfast at André's suite. It's been a while since André and Guillaume have been accompanied. They really enjoy Gaby, Raphael, and Michelle's presence. Raphael has a lot of fun stories about their family. André is also excited to know more about Gaby's life through the people closest to her.

Gaby no longer has a fever. She is ready to practice. Her appetite is also back. She sometimes notices André glancing at her. Is it because he is worried about her health or something else? She also sometimes glances at André. He is so good looking in his v-neck cardigan and white shirt.

"Do you guys like to ski?" Guillaume asks in the middle of breakfast.

"Yes we do. I am the best. Gaby and Michelle are just so-so," Raphael says confidently. Gaby and Michelle only shrug.

"Wanna join us for skiing after the concert? We are going skiing this Sunday at the Grand Massif. It's only an hour drive from here," Guillaume continues.

"That sounds nice. I have never been to the Grand Massif. We always go to the Rocky Mountains or Zermatt for serious skiing. Count me in. I'd like to try something new. How about you Gabs and Michelle?" Raphael asks.

"I am in. It's been a while since I skied," Michelle says.

"I am in too."

"Great. We can leave early in the morning and come back at night. And we will fly to New York on Monday morning," André says.

After breakfast, Raphael and Michelle decide to go around the city for sightseeing. Gaby would love to join them but she wants to practice first. She would rather go sightseeing after she is fully ready for the concert. Otherwise, the sightseeing would not be fun.

André decides to stay and practice as well, but Guillaume decides to join Raphael and Michelle. Guillaume seems to be interested in Michelle. He has seen her perform ballet. Michelle was flattered when he told her that.

After Raphael, Michelle, and Guillaume leave, it is only André and Gaby in the room. Gaby walks towards the window and enjoys the view of Lake Leman. She can see Jet d'Eau, a landmark fountain of Geneva. This is her first time in Geneva. She has been to Switzerland before, but she always stayed in Zurich or Zermatt in the past. Geneva in winter is very pretty. Everything is white. She can see some snow on top of the old buildings in the city. The snow also covers some pedestrian paths and the streets. It's cold, but very pretty and very peaceful.

"I am glad that you are feeling better," André says, suddenly appearing behind her.

"Thank you for the upgrade and for everything else."

"No problem. And please, let me know if you are feeling uncomfortable. I don't want to put too much pressure on you."

"Oh yes. I am feeling okay now. I am pretty confident with the Nocturne piece that I will be playing this Saturday."

"Great. How about for the one in New York?"

"I have not decided yet. Do you have any preference?" Gaby asks.

"I always include Etudes in all my performances, because they are fun and thrilling to watch. Which Chopin's Etude are you comfortable playing?"

"Is Op. 25 No. 1 okay?"

"Yes, that's perfect. I think I can put you in right after the intermezzo."

"Ok great. How about yourself? Are you ready for your concert?"

"For this Saturday, yes, I will be mostly playing chill and relaxing Waltzes and Nocturnes. But for the one in New York, I will be playing Piano Concerto No. 1 and 2 with the New York Philharmonic Orchestra. I want to be absolutely ready and confident with those pieces."

"Oh yes, I know about that! Performing with the New York Philharmonic Orchestra in Carnegie Hall is such a great opportunity."

"Yes, exactly. And you will play in front of them too. If you become a concert pianist, at least they will have seen you perform."

"It seems like you have already planned ahead for my career. I still have to think about what I actually want to do in life. That's also why I took this vacation."

"I see. Take your time to make a decision. I am just giving you options." He smiles.

Gaby starts practicing. André is watching her from the couch. After she finishes the scales and the Nocturne, he gives some feedback on how to improve certain parts. He also plays it for Gaby to give an example. Gaby feels small. When André played the Nocturne, it sounded very different than when she played it. But she does not want to feel insecure. She will learn from André, not be intimidated by him.

When they are in the middle of the discussion, André's phone rings. He looks at the caller ID and suddenly tenses up. "Sorry, I have to take this call. Please continue practicing." André leaves the living room.

"*Bonjour*, Charmaine," André greets the caller.

"*Bonjour* André. It's been a long time. How are you?" Charmaine says. It's been almost a year since he heard her voice. They have not contacted each other since their break up. What does she want now?

"*Bien, merci. Et toi?*"

"*Bien, merci.* Are you in Geneva right now?"

"Yes I am. How do you know?"

"Of course I know. I also know that you will be performing at Victoria Hall this Saturday."

"What do you need Charmaine?" André asks straightforwardly.

"I heard that you have a piano student and that she is performing with you."

"That's correct." André is not interested in explaining further.

"I was wondering if I can perform with you as well. Just one piece."

André does not reply right away. He does not like to change his concert program at the last minute like this. But at the same time, he also knows that Charmaine is a talented cellist. And a performance with her can add value to the concert as well.

"Are you in Geneva right now?"

"Yes. I plan to attend your concert actually."

"What piece do you have in mind?"

"How about Cello Sonata in G minor Op. 65?" Charmaine asks. André knows that the sonata is about fifteen minutes long.

"I only have a slot for five minutes."

"Then we can do one movement only."

"How about the third?" André suggests the Largo movement as it is the most beautiful and the piano is not difficult for him.

"Okay. When can we practice together?"

"When are you available?"

"How about now?" Charmaine asks. André is reluctant. He wants to spend more time with Gaby first.

"I cannot now. How about at two?"

"Sounds good to me. Where do we meet?"

"Let's meet at Beau Rivage."

"Alright. Thanks André. See you soon."

When André returns, his face looks more tense than before. He looks a bit annoyed. Gaby stops playing and asks, "Is everything okay?"

"Yeah, it's just my friend. She wants to perform with me this Saturday."

"Oh really? Does she play piano as well?"

"No, she plays cello." André answers. Gaby tries to connect the dots. She only knows one person who plays cello and knows André. Charmaine. She dares herself to ask.

"Is she Charmaine Lacroix?" Gaby asks. André looks surprised.

"How do you know?"

"Well, I heard in the news that you two used to date before. Are you guys still dating?" Gaby feels a bit jealous. In the past, when André was only her idol, she felt nothing when she discovered that André was dating someone. She even supported them. But it is a different story now. She and André have now become friends.

"No. We are not. That was the first time she made contact after we broke up," André says.

"I see."

"So since you are part of the concert too, I need your approval. Do you mind if she performs one piece this Saturday? I told her I would only give her five minutes."

"You don't need my approval. But yes, of course I agree. She is a talented cellist. I have listened to her too."

"Are you her fan, too?"

"After she broke up with you, no," Gaby answers honestly. André laughs. "You are funny. Anyway, okay. So she will come at around two. How about we finish our practice, have lunch at noon, and then come back here for two. I can introduce you to her."

"Sounds good." Deep inside Gaby feels a stab of jealousy, but she has to control her emotions. André is not her boyfriend. So far they are only good friends. She is not sure of his feelings towards her either. He only hugged her once. And a hug does not mean anything. A friend can give hugs too. She does not want to expect too much. Expectation makes her hurt.

They continue to practice individually. Gaby has returned to her suite to practice too. Suddenly, André has more limited time to practice and to spend with her because of Charmaine. Gaby wishes that they were still doing a duet like back in Auckland. Unfortunately, Gaby will have to watch André do a duet with someone else.

Chapter 19

Wednesday Afternoon
Casanova Restaurant

André and Gaby enjoy lunch at Casanova Restaurant. As usual, they choose a seat beside the window so that they can enjoy the view of Lake Leman. The restaurant is only a few minutes walk from Beau Rivage.

"So how's the practice going? Sorry I ended up practicing by myself. I have to review the piece I am going to play with Charmaine." André asks while they are enjoying their pasta.

"That's okay. I think I am comfortable with the Nocturne. After lunch I am going to start practicing the Etude for the New York concert."

"Great. You play really well, Gaby. I want you to realize that."

"Thanks. Are you excited to perform with Charmaine?" Gaby is curious how their relationship is right now.

"She is a great cellist. I prefer not to stay in touch with my ex, but as a professional, I want to be objective. If she was a stranger, I would probably have said yes to her offer."

"I see." Gaby thought that performing with André was something special. Apparently, André will just perform with anyone that he thinks is competent. Not just Gaby. She feels a little bit disappointed.

"Can I ask you something personal, Gaby?"

"Yes."

"Are you in a relationship right now?" André blushes a little bit when asking that question. Gaby did not expect that.

"No. You? Why do you ask?"

"I am not in a relationship right now. I am just curious. I mean, if you end up being a concert pianist, being in a relationship will take more effort because you will be travelling constantly. I just want to give you a heads up about that."

"I see. Is that why you and Charmaine broke up?" Gaby asks.

"Kind of. She said I was too busy with my concerts and my firm and never had time for her."

"Oh I am sorry. Are you still upset? You don't have to talk about this if you are not comfortable."

"That's okay. I am no longer upset. But yeah, there was nothing else to talk about. Her priorities changed, and so did mine."

"I see. I am not an expert in relationships. So I don't know how to express my sympathy," Gaby says honestly.

"You have never been in a relationship before?"

"Only once. In high school. It only lasted six months."

"And after that, none?" André fishes.

"No. I guess I don't have time. In university, I was busy studying. Right after I graduated, I was busy working and studying for my CPA designation."

"Oh I see. It's good that you are pursuing your dreams first. That way you know more about yourself, your life goals, priorities, and values. Then, when it is the time for a relationship, you know what you are looking for, what you like, and what you don't like," André says. Gaby digests André's words. He is right. Right now, she is in the middle of exploring what she wants to do in her life as well as her values. She agrees that getting to know yourself first before starting a relationship is important. When you don't know yourself, there will be a lot of self-doubt and insecurities. And then, you would start looking for validation from other people. And if you don't receive it, it may hurt your feelings.

"Do you already know yourself, André? I guess you must. You are twenty nine years old."

"I am still exploring myself too right now."

"But can you imagine yourself doing something else other than piano?"

"No. I think being a professional musician is what I want. From what I learned, we can live a meaningful life when we are doing what we like, what we are good at, and what is valuable for other people."

"You have already done that with piano, haven't you?"

"I feel like I haven't added that much value to other people through my music. I don't know if that means I should compose more or do more concerts. I don't know yet. But I haven't been fully satisfied. Maybe there will be no full satisfaction at the end."

"But you have already done something valuable though. A lot of people are touched by your music. You motivate and inspire people. And you have been giving me the opportunity to perform with you."

"Yes, I feel satisfied by doing that. However, I am too greedy. I always want more and more. Maybe after you perform, I want you to be a concert pianist as well, etc." André says. "How about you, Gaby? What do you want to achieve in life?"

"I am kind of enjoying my self-discovery process right now. I know I am twenty five, but there is no rush. I am just grateful for where I am now. I have a good job. Maybe I don't enjoy it that much but at least I can say I am good at it."

"I think that is what I am lacking. Being grateful. I have a comfortable life and I do what I enjoy. I always focus on achieving my next goal and forget to be grateful of what I have accomplished so far. Thanks for reminding me of that."

They continue their deep conversation. They learn from each other by sharing their thoughts and asking each other reflective questions that enable them to learn more about themselves. Both of them feel that their conversation is always meaningful and natural. They are comfortable opening up to each other. For sure they feel compatibility and chemistry. And none of them think that there is any need to rush their relationship to the next steps. They just go with the flow.

*

Wednesday Afternoon
Beau Rivage

They walk back to Beau Rivage reluctantly because Charmaine will arrive soon. It is not yet two, but Charmaine is already waiting for André in the lobby, with her cello case on her shoulder. It is the first time Gaby meets Charmaine in person. She is very beautiful. She is tall and slim, and she has blonde hair. A Barbie-type girl. She is twenty-nine years old, just like André, but she looks more mature. She dresses up very elegantly, too. Gaby feels like she is a kid compared to Charmaine.

"*Salut* André!" Charmaine looks so happy to see him. She quickly kisses André on both cheeks. Gaby is a bit surprised but she remembers that that's a custom in France and in Quebec.

"*Salut* Charmaine," André says politely. Gaby notices that André is not as enthusiastic as Charmaine.

"Let me introduce you two. Gaby, this is Charmaine. Charmaine, this is Gaby. Gaby can speak French," André explains.

"*Bonjour. Enchantée.*"

"*Enchantée*, Gaby," Charmaine replies.

Her first impression of Charmaine is that she is pretty mature and polite too. What a perfect lady! They go up to André's suite. Charmaine and Gaby talk about how long they have been playing their instruments, etc.

Then, they arrive at André's suite. Gaby goes back to her suite, which is beside André's suite and only separated by a door. She will continue practicing her Nocturne and the Aeolian Harp Etude. She does not want to think about anything else other than her music.

"Are you guys dating?" Charmaine asks André directly. She is taking her cello out of the case.

"No," André replies shortly.

"I am relieved. She is beautiful," Charmaine says. André does not comment. Today, he does not want to discuss personal matters with Charmaine. Today is purely for practicing.

"Let's tune your cello."

"Alright."

They practice for about two hours. Charmaine seems to have mastered the piece really well. It seems that she has been practicing a lot.

"What do you think?" Charmaine asks after they finish their practice.

"I think it went really well."

"Great. When will we practice again?"

"I think you are pretty much ready to perform. We can just meet on Friday. I will be doing a final rehearsal at Victoria Hall."

"I want to practice again tomorrow."

André is trying to plan his schedule in his head. He still has to practice for his own pieces for this Saturday and two Piano Concertos for the concert in New York. Not to mention that he wants to be available for Gaby in case she needs his guidance. He wants to spend time with Gaby. And he also has to catch up with work.

"I think you are ready. We don't need to practice tomorrow," André says. Charmaine is silent for a while.

"Are you avoiding me?"

"I am not. If I was avoiding you, I would not have agreed to be your accompanist and allowed you to perform in my concert," André says. Charmaine examines his face.

"Why are you so cold to me? I know that we are no longer in a relationship, but you don't need to change like this."

"I haven't changed. I am what I am."

"Is it because of Gaby? You like her, don't you?"

"Charmaine, let me remind you that I am just your accompanist now. I prefer not to discuss private matters."

"I cannot hold it anymore. I miss you André! I regret the decision I made. Can we start all over again?" Charmaine takes a closer step towards André. André is surprised, and he does not know what to say. He remembers those five years they were together. They were very happy. But at that time, they were dating because André needed her, and she needed him too. André used to care about her. But now his feelings have changed.

"I am sorry Charmaine. I appreciated what you did for me throughout our five years together, but it was all in the past. I have decided to move on," André says honestly.

"You don't need to decide now. Think about it over the next few days." Charmaine packs her cello and then leaves.

When Gaby is practicing from her suite, she can hear André and Charmaine's music faintly. It sounds very beautiful. She cannot help to feel that she wishes it was her who was practicing with André. But again, instead of feeling jealous, she focuses on her own music. She even plays it better due to her current emotional state. But imagining André and Charmaine playing a duet together and looking very compatible hurts Gaby to some extent. She doesn't like being emotional like this. So, she ends up pouring her emotion into the piano. And it works. She feels like the music is consoling her soul.

Suddenly, she hears a knock. "Come in."

André comes in. He looks very tired. Gaby is wondering what is going on.

"How's your practice?" André asks.

"Good. How's yours? Has Charmaine left already?"

"Yes. The practice with her was good. We are going to practice again on Friday. You should also do a final rehearsal with us on Friday," André says. When André referred to him and Charmaine as "us", Gaby was a bit disappointed.

"For sure."

"I also wanted to tell you that I will be busy practicing and working until Saturday. But if you need anything, please let me know. Just come to my suite or text me. Okay?" André says. Gaby nods. She is wondering if André reconciled his relationship with Charmaine and maybe that's why he will be so busy? With practicing, work, and Charmaine. Is this his polite way of saying that he no longer has time for her? Gaby does not want to imagine things that only put her down.

"Okay," Gaby says.

"Good luck practicing, Gaby. You will do awesome." André smiles and then leaves.

Chapter 20

Thursday Afternoon
Geneva

That day, Gaby decides to go sightseeing with Raphael, Michelle, and Guillaume. She practiced for three hours in the morning and will take a break for the rest of the day. Since tomorrow she will be practicing at Victoria Hall, Saturday is the performance day, and Sunday is the ski day, today is the only day she can go sightseeing around Geneva.

She hasn't seen André nor communicated with him since yesterday. She heard him practicing until nine yesterday but after that she didn't know what he was doing. He also skipped dinner. Apparently, Raphael, Michelle, and Guillaume got along really well and they had an amazing day yesterday. They went to CERN, St. Pierre Cathedral, and Palais des Nations. Guillaume has visited Geneva several times before and he became Raphael and Michelle's tour guide.

There was only a slight tension between Raphael and Guillaume yesterday when they compared Montreal Canadiens and Toronto Maple Leaf hockey teams. Raphael also complained about the French language in Quebec that just added extra work for everybody. Guillaume complained about how they never served real poutine in Ontario. Until Michelle had to remind them that whichever provinces that they live in, they are all Canadians. That seemed to hit Raphael and Guillaume. After that, they became more bonding and just teased each other occasionally.

Gaby is glad that she will join them today for sightseeing. She does not want to think about André and Charmaine. At least today's trip can distract her from André. They start with a boat cruise sail around Lake

Leman. Luckily the lake is not frozen in the winter, unlike Lake Ontario or the beautiful lakes in Alberta. From the boat, they can see the Jet d'Eau closer. The fountain is very tall from up close. After the cruise, they continue walking along Rue du Rhone. Gaby really likes Geneva. The city is very beautiful. There are many old and historical buildings. If she wanted to pick a place for retirement, Geneva would probably be the best. The atmosphere is very calm and relaxing.

Michelle suggests that they sit in a coffee shop just to have a chat and relax.

"How's the practice, Gabs?" Guillaume asks.

"It is good. I feel more confident with the piece that I will be playing for this Saturday, because the tempo is slower."

"Glad to hear. André must be very proud."

"I still don't understand why André agreed to perform with Charmaine. They broke up, didn't they?" Michelle comments.

"Yes. Well, my guess is André agreed with it because he feels guilty."

"Guilty about what?" Raphael asks. He becomes interested in the gossip as well.

"Right after they graduated from the Conservatoire de Paris, Charmaine came to Montreal with André because they were dating. But in Montreal, Charmaine was not very successful. Had she stayed in Paris, she would have had a better chance of being a successful cellist."

"Oh, I see. But it was Charmaine's own decision right? It's not like André forced her to move to Montreal with him?" Michelle asks.

"The situation was a bit complicated. André's parents had just passed away at that time. André had to return to Montreal. So

Charmaine knew if they wanted to continue their relationship, she had no choice other than to move to Montreal with him."

"Does André still have feelings towards Charmaine?" Michelle asks something that Gaby is also curious about.

"I am not sure about that. André is a very private person. Even to me. But he never brought up Charmaine since they broke up," Guillaume explains. He turns towards Gaby, "In fact, I have a feeling that André is into you, Gaby." Guillaume looks at her meaningfully.

"Me? Oh, I am not sure. We definitely enjoy each other's company. We like practicing piano, and having conversations about music and about life. I don't know if he wants to be more than a friend."

"For someone like André to open up to someone is very rare. As I said, he is very introverted. He only opens up to someone he is comfortable with. So I think you have earned his trust. That's a good start," Guillaume says.

"But why has he not made any move with Gaby though? He hasn't, has he, Gabs?" Raphael asks.

"Raphael, c'mon..." Gaby feels uncomfortable discussing André with Guillaume. No matter what, Guillaume is André's best friend.

"About that, André is probably focusing on his concert first. Maybe wait to see how it will turn out after New York."

"Well, aren't you and André going back to Montreal after the tour ends? We will go back to Toronto." Michelle says.

"Guys, let's talk about something else. I am not comfortable talking about André like this," Gaby says.

"Okay. One last thing, André is someone difficult to read. So you can just be open with him first. And just trust him. I have known him for a while and I know that he is very trustworthy," Guillaume adds.

*

Thursday Evening
Beau Rivage

André has practiced for more than six hours. He practiced the Etudes for three hours in the morning, and then had lunch, and then practiced the Piano Concertos for another three hours after lunch. He has just finished his dinner and is about to practice the Waltzes and Nocturnes that he will be playing this Saturday.

He realizes that the repertoire in Geneva matches his mood right now. The Waltz and Nocturne pieces that he picked all sound melancholy. He is experiencing a lonely night again. He misses Gaby even though it has been only a day. For some reasons, he feels that Auckland is a more romantic city than Geneva. Maybe it is because he was less busy in Auckland and had more time to spend with Gaby.

He knows that Gaby was practicing this morning. He can feel that her playing has improved so much. She will also be playing one of the Nocturnes and she played it with a sad mood that was very touching. André is wondering if that is how she truly feels right now or she is just so good at altering her own feelings.

He hears Guillaume enter the room. Guillaume looks so happy and fresh recently. André bets that it is because he has just made new friends with Raphael, Michelle, and Gaby.

"How's your day going?" André asks.

"Really good! We went on a boat cruise and then explored the Rue du Rhone," Guillaume says while he is taking off his jacket.

"I am jealous."

"How's your practice?"

"Good."

"Non-stop since the morning?"

"Kind of. I am taking breaks every three hours. I have only been practicing for eight hours in total."

"Maybe it's time to rest for the rest of the day?" Guillaume suggests. He knows that André can be extremely hardworking sometimes. Especially when he is in the mood.

"Yeah, maybe."

André decides to end the practice and goes upstairs to get his laptop to start working on Gauthier Capital. In the middle of the stairs he suddenly feels out of breath and dizzy. 'Oh, not again please,' he says to himself. He forgets that climbing stairs can be this challenging. It's probably because he has been sitting at the piano for too long. Again, he feels like the room is spinning so he gets down on his knees and grabs the handrail so that he does not fall.

"Are you okay, André?" Guillaume approaches him right away and helps him to stand. He looks very worried.

"Can you please help me walk to the bed?" André asks. He feels like his chest is being squeezed from the inside and he coughs a few times. Guillaume puts André's right arm on his shoulder, grabs André's waist, and helps him to the bed. André lies down for a while when trying to catch his breath. He puts two pillows under his head so that he can breathe easier.

"I will call a doctor now," Guillaume says as he takes his phone from his pocket.

"Let's not do that. There is nothing the doctor can do. Not until I finish my concert tour," André says. Guillaume sighs. "We still have ten days until your concert ends and two weeks until we go back to Montreal. Your condition is worsening."

"Two weeks. I can survive for the next two weeks." André closes his eyes to try to distract himself from his irregular and fast heartbeat.

"Okay. Anything I can do for you in the meantime?"

"Yes, don't tell Gaby or anyone else about this."

Chapter 21

Friday Afternoon
Victoria Hall

Victoria Hall is located at Rue du General-Dufour. The moment she enters the concert hall, Gaby falls in love with the place right away. Victoria Hall was built in 1894, so it has a very antique décor. It is unlike the other concert halls she has attended in the past. This concert hall feels like home because it is smaller and more private.

Charmaine is already on the stage practicing by herself. She is playing her cello beautifully.

"Hi guys!" Charmaine stops playing when she sees André, Guillaume and Gaby approaching the stage.

"Hi Charmaine, long time no see!" Guillaume approaches her and they greet each other by giving kisses on both cheeks.

"Guillaume! How are you? It's really nice to see you!" Charmaine seems genuinely happy to see Guillaume.

"I am good. Thanks! How about you?"

"Good thanks." They catch up with each other for a while.

"Ready for the practice, Gaby?" André asks her. André seems a bit quiet. He looks pale and tired as well. Gaby is wondering if he is sick.

"Yes, I am. You?"

"Me too."

"You don't look well. Are you feeling okay?" Gaby asks worriedly.

"Yes I am okay. I am just tired. Too much practicing and working. Thanks for asking though."

"Let me know if I can help with anything." Gaby sincerely wants to make André feel better.

"Thank you. I appreciate it. I guess I will practice with Charmaine, and then I will go next, and then you can practice as long as you want after me. How does that sound?"

"Sounds good."

After Guillaume and Charmaine finish catching up, André walks towards the piano on the stage and they start practicing. Guillaume sits beside Gaby in the front row. They listen to André and Charmaine playing. They both sound very awesome. What a perfect duet.

"Wow. They play from heart to heart with each other. It's impressive. The music is full of emotion," Gaby says.

"I prefer the one that you played with André. It was livelier and gave off a positive emotion. This one is sadder," Guillaume comments.

Apparently, it is not only the Cello Sonata Largo that creates the sad atmosphere. The rest of André's repertoire for the concert in Geneva sounds very melancholy, too. It is very different when he plays now versus when he played in Auckland. In Auckland, he played vibrantly. Now, he is more subdued. Charmaine is listening to André not far from where Guillaume and Gaby sit.

"Is André feeling okay, Guillaume? He does not look too well," Gaby asks.

"He is just tired. Practicing the whole day, and working during night. We normally only travelled within Europe or Asia. But now, we travel across the globe."

"I see."

After an hour, André finishes his practice and Gaby walks to the stage. She sees Charmaine rise from her seat and walk towards André. "I need to talk to you. Would you mind having a coffee with me across the street?"

André is thinking for a second. He actually wants to reject Charmaine's invitation because he prefers to watch Gaby's practice. But even though Charmaine is his ex, he still respects her and it would not be nice if he rejected her in front of Guillaume and Gaby.

"Sure." André says to Charmaine. "Give me one second."

André walks towards Gaby. "Are you okay practicing by yourself?"

"Yes, I am okay. You can go."

"Call or text me if you need anything."

"Yes, thank you."

Then André walks towards Guillaume, "Can you please watch over Gaby? I am going to go with Charmaine for a while."

"Sure. Have fun," Guillaume says.

André leaves with Charmaine and Gaby cannot help but to feel jealous. They look very good and very compatible with each other. Like a mature couple. The only way she can console herself is by pouring her emotions into the piano.

*

Friday Afternoon
Coffee Shop, Geneva

"What do you want, Charmaine?" André asks when they have ordered their coffee and sit by the window inside the café.

"I just want to talk with you. Have you considered what I proposed last time?"

"You mean for us to resume our relationship?"

"Yes."

"Sorry, but I have to say no. It did not work between us. You live in Paris and I live in Montreal."

"I will move to Montreal," Charmaine insists.

"Last time you did that, and it still did not work."

"Last time I realized that I was so selfish. I wanted your attention and I wanted my career as a cellist to be successful too. And when I did not get both, I thought it would not work between us. But for this past year, I realized that you don't need to give me your attention or your time and I don't need my career as long as I am with you. You are more important than my career," Charmaine says.

"Thank you for your honesty, Charmaine. Unfortunately, I cannot start over with you."

"But why? Do you fall in love with someone else? It's Gaby, isn't it?"

"Yes."

*

Friday Evening
Beau Rivage

That night Gaby is practicing again in her suite. She practices back and forth between the Aeolian Harp that she will be playing in New York and the Nocturne that she will be playing tomorrow. She wants to play like a professional so that even though someone calls her an amateur again, she will not be affected because she is confident with her skills.

Even though she starts to enjoy practicing and performing, she cannot deny that she is looking forward to this concert to end. They still have one more week in New York after this. She cannot imagine how André manages it. Gaby only plays one short piece every performance. But André has to perform at least seven pieces and some of them can last twenty minutes. With only one week gap between concerts, it must be very tiring. Therefore, Gaby decides that she has to be independent. She cannot keep bugging him with questions or keep asking him for feedback every time she plays a piece. She wants to give him some time for himself.

However, every time she is not with André, she misses him so much. He is just beside the door but beyond reach. She can hear him practicing. She wants to make sure that he is fine and he is making progress with his practice and work. If he looks stressed or depressed, she wants to hug him like back in Piha Beach. She wants to give him comfort. She wants what is best for him even though it may not be the best for her. If Charmaine is the only woman who has the privilege of being by his side, she will accept that. If André does not reciprocate her feelings, she can live with that as long as he is happy. Has her crush developed into love?

André is practicing his pieces in his suite again. He feels bad about Charmaine but he cannot force his feelings. His heart only has a spot for one person, which is Gaby.

He misses her so much when they are not together. She is just beside the door but beyond reach. He hears her practicing now and he wants her to focus on her practice. He does not want to bug her. He wants her to discover her own playing style that she feels comfortable with. He said this afternoon at Victoria Hall that if she needed any help, she could just call or text him. But Gaby is very independent and she has neither called nor texted him until now. That only makes André more proud of her. She can survive without him. She is a very tough girl, even though it was just last week that a spectator humiliated her. But she keeps going.

A conversation with Charmaine this afternoon triggered something he has not really thought about before. He realizes that his feeling towards Gaby is more than a fling or crush.

He has fallen in love with Gaby.

He knows that he has only known her for two weeks. However, as a trained musician, he feels and interprets his surroundings deeply. This is why he can fall in love quickly. But he does not feel naïve. He just wants to enjoy and accept the feelings. And with this concert tour, there are few distractions between him and Gaby. Only Charmaine. So Gaby is the one who has occupied his mind for the past two weeks. It feels natural for him to fall in love with her.

If he is able to start a relationship or even a family, he will want someone like Gaby beside him. She is smart, tough, talented, and gentle at the same time. He wants to make sure that Gaby is fine and she is making progress with her practice. Whenever she feels anxious, sad, or sick, he wants to be the person who comforts her. He wants what is best for her even though it may not be the best for him. The only reason he has not made a move yet is because of his health right now. He wants her to be with a man who is capable of taking care of her, even though it may not be him. But he can live with that as long as she is happy.

Chapter 22

Saturday Evening
Victoria Hall

The seats at Victoria Hall are all full tonight. Gaby is ready to perform but she is still nervous. Now she accepts that being nervous is normal and is part of performing. However, based on her experience, when she is on stage, she is no longer nervous but is instead enjoying her music. Gaby is looking forward to that.

Today, André is wearing a white shirt, black suit jacket without tie, and black pants. He looks more relaxed today but the spotlight that focuses on him makes his melancholic expression and melancholic mood more visible on the stage. Nonetheless, he still looks very cool and sensitive. His emotion appears very deep and vulnerable. The repertoire for today is as follows:

Chopin – Etude in E flat Major Op. 10 No. 11 (Arpeggio)
Chopin – Waltz in A minor Op. 34 No. 2
Chopin – Waltz in C-Sharp minor Op. 64 No. 2
Chopin – Waltz in F minor Op. 70 No. 2
Chopin – Cello Sonata in G minor Op. 65: III Largo
˜Intermezzo ˜
Chopin – Nocturne in B-flat minor Op. 9 No. 1
Chopin – Nocturne in C-Sharp minor Op. 27 No. 1
Chopin – Nocturne in D-flat Major Op. 27 No. 2
Chopin – Nocturne in C minor Op. 48 No. 1
Chopin – Nocturne in E Major Op. 62 No. 2

Chopin – Nocturne in E minor Op. Posth 72 No. 1
Chopin – Nocturne in C-Sharp minor Op. Posth.
Chopin – Op. 22: Andante spianato

For the first session, as usual, she will enjoy André's performance from the audience seat with Raphael, Michelle, and Guillaume. Today, André's performance is more relaxed than in the previous concerts. The pieces may not be technically challenging (except for the Etude), however, the challenge would be in the musical interpretation. It is by no means easy to tell the story to the audience through these pieces. The tempo is also important because if you are playing it too slowly, the audience may not be able to connect the story within a piece. But if you are playing it too fast, the audience may not be able to enjoy the emotion behind it. So, it requires the appropriate balance.

André is definitely a genius in musical interpretation in addition to technique. His technique is definitely flawless, but moreover, his musical interpretation is very deep. The Waltzes that he picked for today's repertoire are mostly from number two and in minor keys, which are slower and sadder than number one or three. However, the music he creates is more than just sad music. There is also a sense of elegance. The combination is complex. He tells a story not only within one piece, but also from one piece to another, and there is an emotional connection. Even Raphael, who always thinks that classical music is boring, seems to get carried away with the emotion as well. André knows how to shape the melody, when to highlight some parts with more forte, and when to soften some parts. His touch on the piano is also very soft and light. When it requires more power, he still controls the tone very well without sounding rough.

From the first concert in Singapore, to Auckland, and now in Geneva, it seems like three different pianists are playing for the concerts. Gaby has no idea how André does that. His personality is very complex and in order to be able to do what he does, it requires deep understanding of the piece, and multiple years of exploration on various Chopin's pieces.

Again, Gaby feels like she learns a lot from André. When she plays the Nocturne later on, she hopes it will sound similar to André's playing. They may interpret the piece differently, but with regards to the lightness, softness, and power, she wants to make her music very beautiful and refined like his.

And then here comes the duet between Charmaine and André. The focus is on Charmaine as André is the accompanist. Charmaine plays it beautifully as well. She is such a talented musician. It is no surprise that André fell in love with her. Her fingers move across the cello strings gently. After they finish playing, the audience gives them a loud applause. It was very different from when Gaby played a duet with André. Gaby cannot help but feel inferior. But she stays strong and gives them a sincere applause.

The Waltzes that he played during the first session and the Nocturnes that he is currently playing represent his mood for this past week perfectly. He is pouring his emotions into the piano. It is not frustration nor anxiety nor anger. It's just loneliness, helplessness, sadness and desperation for love in the midst of the luxurious and elegant life that he has. He tries to convey that to the audience.

André wants Gaby. He wants to live a long life to be beside her forever. But can he? When he plays the Nocturnes, he imagines lonely nights he spent without Gaby. The beautiful Geneva, Lake Leman, street lights that illuminate the city at night, his luxurious suite at Beau Rivage that feels empty without Gaby... Will Gaby meet someone who can guide her in her journey to become a professional musician? And if one day Gaby becomes like him, will she experience loneliness too?

During the intermezzo earlier, he saw Gaby in the dressing room. She looks very beautiful in her pink dress and soft make up. She looks very pure and vulnerable, but there is strength inside her. Now she is listening to him playing from the dressing room by herself. He wants his music to reach her particularly. He wants them to embrace the same feelings and emotions.

He finishes playing his last Nocturne before Gaby's Nocturne. The audience gives him a big applause when he bows, and then he leaves the stage. He sees Gaby stand on the side of the stage. He looks at her in the eyes with conviction, taps her shoulder and nods to give encouragement. He does not need to say a word, Gaby knows what he means. She nods back with determination and walks to the stage.

She bows and the audience gives her applause. André is not playing but his heart is pounding again. He can sense both Gaby's nervousness and self-determination, as it is himself who experiences it. But when Gaby starts playing, all the nervousness is gone. André is surprised.

It is like listening to himself playing!

She plays the notes very softly and gently. There is desperation and loneliness too. But she maintains the elegance of the piece. How can this be? Is she feeling the same thing as he feels? He feels her pain. Gaby, what makes you feel this?

That night, not only André, but also Raphael, Michelle, Guillaume, Charmaine, and the audience feel the power of their music. Two different people with different backgrounds can play and interpret the music the same way. It creates a harmonious feeling.

Chapter 23

Saturday Evening
Quai du Mont-Blanc outside Beau Rivage

Gaby cannot describe her feelings for the past three hours. She has tried her best to deliver a beautiful performance. And when she finished, the audience gave her a big applause. Some of them even gave her a standing applause! She appreciated that of course, however, what was more important for her was that today, she played whole-heartedly and went deeper into the music. That made her happier and more satisfied than the mere applause.

Now she is enjoying the beautiful night at the pier in front of her hotel. She hugs herself because it is three degree below out there. Even though that is nothing compared to the winter in Toronto. She reflects on what has happened after her performance.

She cannot forget André's reaction after she played the Nocturne. His face was not only full of surprise but also proud and admiring. He did not say much other than, "That was very powerful and touching, Gaby. Thank you." But his expression and gesture were more than words. Gaby did not say a word. She walked directly towards him and hugged him tight. She did not care what he would think. She was just full of emotion after playing that Nocturne. She buried her head in his chest and she could smell his masculine and comforting scent. She did not want to let him go. This hug represented her gratitude and appreciation towards him, who inspired and pushed Gaby to get deeper into her music. Gaby discovered more about her own emotions and his emotions.

André did not react at first. He was probably surprised and not expecting a hug from Gaby. Gaby could hear his heart was beating faster after she hugged him. Gaby could feel her heart pounding too. Then, she could feel that he hugged her back tightly. And he caressed her head gently. That simple gesture meant a lot for Gaby. She could feel his support physically and emotionally. She felt warm with his arms wrapped around her.

The hug only lasted thirty seconds and then André had to go back to the stage to perform his last piece. And while Gaby was standing there, Charmaine appeared from behind her.

"That was a beautiful performance, Gaby," Charmaine said sincerely. Gaby was wondering if Charmaine saw that she hugged André. But there was no hostility in Charmaine's words.

"Thank you. So was your performance," Gaby replied.

"I have never seen André like that before. His performance is also different since he met you, I think. You two are very compatible," Charmaine said. Gaby did not know what to say. But if there was something between André and Charmaine, she did not want to be a third person.

"That's because we practiced together often and I have been listening to him since I was five. Before you misunderstand, nothing is happening between us. We are just friends or mentor-mentee you can say," Gaby explained.

Charmaine laughed. "I asked André to resume our relationship," Charmaine confessed honestly. Gaby was surprised. She felt like someone just stabbed her chest. She also felt like she was hit in the stomach.

"But he rejected me," Charmaine continued. Gaby felt so relieved.

"Why?"

"Because he is in love with someone else."

Gaby did not know what to say. She crossed her fingers. "With who?"

"You may want to hear it from himself. I wish you the best of luck Gaby. André is a good person."

And then Charmaine left.

Gaby returns from her reverie to present time. Tonight is very beautiful. She just wants to experience the night in Geneva outside of her suite.

Then she feels that someone is approaching her from behind.

André.

He smiles at her and offers her coffee in a paper cup. He carries another cup on his other hand. They have not seen each other after the performance as Guillaume and André needed to take care of some paperwork at Victoria Hall for a while. André texted her earlier to let her know that she can go back to the hotel with Raphael and Michelle first. Then he added that they would celebrate the success of the performance back in the hotel. After she arrived at the hotel, she did not feel like staying inside after what happened. She needed some time to think. She wanted to be alone and enjoy the night by herself. Or even better, with André.

"How are you feeling, Gaby?" André asks. He is still wearing his suit from the concert.

"Better than last time," Gaby says. She drinks her coffee. Her hands feel warmer thanks to the hot coffee.

"I cannot be prouder of you," André says.

"Thanks. This is all thanks to you."

They enjoy the night in silence for a while. And suddenly, the snow falls. What can be prettier than this? Enjoying the night, the beautiful city, the lake, and the snowfall with André. The atmosphere is very peaceful.

André steps closer towards her and takes the jacket hoodie behind her head to put it over her head so that the snow does not fall directly into her head. Gaby looks at him. André himself is only wearing his suit, which does not have a hoodie. The snow falls directly on his brown hair. He shivers in the cold.

"Do you want to go inside? You can get sick without a warm jacket."

"I am okay. Are you cold?"

"No."

"Then let's stay here for a while," André says. They continue enjoying the night in silence. After several days of uncertainty and doubts about André's feelings towards her, tonight she feels closer again to him. Deep inside, she thanks Charmaine for clarifying the situation between her and André.

André suddenly offers his hands. It looks like he wants to hold her hands. She moves her coffee to her left hand and holds André's hand with her free right hand. His hand feels cold. So does her hand. But with their skin against each other, it starts getting warmer. It feels very nice to be able to hold hands like this. With André Gauthier-Lee himself. It feels unreal to Gaby.

"Gaby, you are very special to me. I want you to be happy," André says sincerely. And then he moves another step closer towards her. Their faces are very close to each other now. She can feel his breath. He puts his arms around her waist.

Then, he kisses her gently on the lips.

Gaby closes her eyes and puts her arms around his neck. She feels warm all over her body. Their bodies are now against each other. He smells very nice. His hug is so warm and his kiss is so gentle. She feels very close to him both physically and emotionally.

Gaby will remember that night for the rest of her life.

Her first kiss with André.

Chapter 24

Sunday Morning
Grand Massif, Haute Savoie, Mont-Blanc, France

That morning, they drive from Geneva to the Grand Massif ski resort in France. The weather is very nice today. Gaby is very excited to go skiing with Raphael, Michelle, André, and Guillaume.

Gaby is still thinking about her first kiss with André yesterday. She thinks that it was very romantic. They kissed for about ten minutes or so, and then they went back to the suite because it started getting cold outside. They went back to their respective suites because André had to go back to work.

When they met again this morning, both of them blushed shyly. André had not made any comments about last night. Like, are they officially in a relationship right now? Or they are just friends now and last night was just two people got carried away with the beautiful and romantic atmosphere? Gaby decides that she will just go with the flow. She does not want to worry too much about their current relationship status. She wants to focus on the concert first and then think about it after. She is pretty sure that André feels the same. The concert in New York will be the most intense concert in this tour as he will be playing two Piano Concertos with the New York Philharmonic Orchestra at Carnegie Hall, while he is also busy with work. Gaby does not want to push him too much. She wants to give him some time to think. But right now, she enjoys spending time with him and getting to know him better first.

They arrive at the ski resort at around ten. Then, they rent the ski equipment in the rental office. Gaby does not ski very often. She used to take ski lessons from school when she was in elementary school. They went skiing in Lake Louise, Alberta a few times, but that was it. Raphael and her dad are the ones who enjoy skiing. Raphael always goes skiing with his friends when his schedule permits it.

The Grand Massif area connects four ski resorts including Les Carroz, Flaine, Morillon, and Samoens. The highest peak is Les Grandes Platieres at 2,480m, which is part of Flaine. But right now they decide to start from Les Carroz with a lower attitude. Especially André and Gaby. They don't want to take a risk skiing in high altitude and difficult slopes to prevent any possible injuries, as they will have a concert six days from now.

They take the chairlift to Tête des Saix. The altitude is 2,118m. At least it also has some challenging slopes including the red and black slopes. Red slopes only exist in Europe and do not exist in North America. The difficulty is between the blue and black slopes. When they arrive at the top of Tête des Saix, the view is incredible. They can see the Alps Mountains all covered in snow. The view is very peaceful. For Gaby, she is more excited in enjoying the view than the skiing itself.

"Alright! Let's race. We'll meet at the base of Tête des Saix near the chairlift, okay?" Raphael fastens his ski helmet and is ready to ski down the advanced black slope.

"Yes!"

They ski down. While Raphael is skiing on the black slope, André and Guillaume choose the red slope. Gaby and Michelle stay on the blue slope. But eventually all the slopes will merge together near the end.

Gaby is surprised that André is actually very good at skiing as well. Is there anything that he cannot do well? Gaby smiles to herself.

She enjoys the adrenaline rush when skiing down the hills. She feels free. It reminds her of some of the virtuoso Chopin's Etudes that André likes to play, such as Waterfall and Ocean. It's thrilling and flowing. Just like what she is experiencing now.

André enjoys the thrill of the adrenaline rush as well. However, by the time they reach the base, he is panting and out of breath. Raphael arrives first, he is second and Guillaume follows him not far behind. Gaby and Michelle are still up there, not visible yet.

"Phew! That was fun!" Raphael cries.

"Agreed!" André replies. He is still trying to catch his breath.

After Gaby and Michelle arrive, they go up again. They try several different trails. André feels excited. It has been a while since the last time he was skiing. It was probably three years ago at Mont Tremblant with Guillaume and Charmaine.

By the third time they go up and down the hill, André already feels satisfied with the adrenaline rush and he wants to have a more relaxed and fun time with Gaby. He rides the chairlift with her and stays on the blue slope with her even though the slope is too easy for him. Once, Gaby and Michelle try the red slope and they find themselves falling multiple times as the slope is very steep and they lose control of the ski. André always stays close to watch over Gaby while Guillaume stays close to Michelle. André smiles looking at Guillaume and Michelle. They look good together.

"You are still doing okay, Gabs?" André checks on her when the red slope finally merges with the blue slope and they can relax a bit.

"Yes! This is exciting even though it is hard," Gaby says. Her cheek is red due to the cold. It reminds André of their kiss last time. The kiss that made him unable to sleep that night.

"I feel like skiing is somewhat like piano too. You fall but rise up again, and your skiing technique becomes better after falling a thousand times. Same thing with piano. You make mistakes here and there, but through mistakes you become a better player." Gaby says

"That's a good analogy. I am glad that you are willing to give another try performing in the concert after what happened in Auckland. Now you see you have improved a lot for the past few days. That is because you are not giving up." André says.

"Thanks to your encouragement. I could not have done it without you."

"As a matter of fact, you should give all the credit to yourself. I did not spend much time with you when you were practicing for the concert in Geneva. I was busy practicing on my own and with Charmaine. But it looked like you could do well without me!" André says enthusiastically.

"What are you talking about? I could come up with the interpretation for that Nocturne thanks to you. I listened to how you played it before my turn." She smiles. He smiles back and caresses her helmet because he cannot caress her head. Gaby likes it when he does that. They continue skiing down the hill together.

It is almost three now and they are all tired. They are back at the top of Tête des Saix, and ready for their last run to the base. This time André, Guillaume, and Raphael stay on the blue slope and they let Gaby and Michelle go first as they are slower. André and Guillaume will go next, and Raphael will go last. It turns out that it is for the best.

It happens in just a split second.

André notices that a skier loses control of his skis when going down the hill. The skier is coming down towards Gaby. He is going too fast and he will collide with Gaby.

Without thinking, André lets go of his ski poles and skis down towards him. His plan is to switch the direction of that skier to the left so that he will not crash into Gaby. But in order to do that, he must crash into that skier himself. This is going to hurt, but he has no choice.

André skis down from the right to left and he purposely bumps into the skier. They fall hard to the left, while Gaby is safe on the right. When they fall, André positions himself so that he falls first so the skier can fall on him, a softer landing spot, rather than on the hard snow. André's reflex is to protect his elbows so he does not break his arms. He cannot play piano with a broken arm. So, he falls hard to the ground on his right side and right shoulder and then he can feel the skier landing hard on the right side of his body.

Because the slope is very steep, André and the skier continue to tumble for at least eight meters before they stop. Their skis come off their feet and left behind.

André does not move for a while. That was a hard fall. He is still too shocked to move.

Raphael and Guillaume look towards André and the skier on the ground with horror. They rush towards them.

"André! Are you okay?" Raphael releases his feet from his ski board so that he can kneel beside André who is still lying on the ground. At least André is conscious. That is a good sign. André tries to nod. He starts to feel the pain on his side as it hit the ground really hard. And he feels pain around his right ribs too, where the skier landed before they tumbled.

"Okay, now grab my hand and try to get up very slowly," Raphael offers his hand.

André does what Raphael says. He grabs Raphael's hand and tries to get up on his knee. Raphael is now helping him steady himself by supporting both of his arms.

Finally André can stand up slowly. The pain in his side becomes more intense. Hopefully it is not broken ribs.

Guillaume and Raphael hold André as he is still unable to stand steadily.

"Hey what are you doing!" The skier who fell with André is now in a sitting position. He looks shocked and tries to understand what happened.

"Hey, you were the one who did not use your eyes! You were about to hit her, you know that right?" Guillaume was annoyed. He points towards Gaby. Gaby and Michelle are several meters below and they stop when they hear a commotion from behind. Gaby, who does not know what happened behind her, looks confused. She looks at André and the skier back and forth. What has happened?

The skier just looks embarrassed. "Is that why he crashed into me on purpose?"

"At least I tried to make you fall on me instead of on the ground," André says. He finally is able to stand steadily.

"You look fine to me. If you would excuse us, I have to check on my friend. He may have broken his ribs. Make sure you call a ski patrol and get checked," Raphael says and then he turns towards André.

"Let's go to the nearest first aid post. Are you able to ski yourself?" Raphael asks. André nods. He is looking for his skis and the poles. They are still 10 meters behind and above him. They ask some other skiers up there to collect them. And then they ski down to the nearest first aid post. André is still shocked but slowly gets himself together. He tries to breathe slowly and deeply. At least he saved his arms.

When they enter the nearest first aid post, Gaby is still digesting what happened. She looks at André worriedly. He looks like he is in pain and he is guarding his right side ribs with his hand. He takes a seat on one of the benches.

"André, in case Gaby has not told you, I am an emergency resident physician. You are going to be fine. I am going to examine you now, okay?" Raphael says. André just nods. Raphael and Guillaume help André remove his jacket and his sweater, and they help him lie down on the bench. They notice that his right shoulder and his right side are slightly red, which indicates blunt trauma. It looks like in a few hours or days it will turn into bruises.

"Do you feel any pain?" Raphael asks.

"Only on my right side and right ribs."

"Okay, just in case, I am going to give you a quick head-to-toe exam first before we come back to your right side. I just want to make sure that there is no internal bleeding or broken bones." André nods again. Fortunately, everything else looks good other than his reddened shoulder and the right side of his body.

"I am going to press against your ribs gently." Raphael continues his exam. André grimaces in pain slightly when Raphael presses his ribs.

"Is it painful?" Raphael asks.

"Not as bad as I thought."

Raphael examines his breathing more carefully. It does not look like André has broken ribs, but his breathing is rapid and shallow.

"Can you take a deep breath and exhale, please?" Raphael observes the chest movement and does not see any sign of flail chest. Another good sign. But he still thinks that there is something wrong.

"Are you done Raphael?" André asks. He is about to get up.

"Hang on. Not yet. Lie back please," Raphael pushes his shoulder gently. And then he turns into Michelle. "Can you find the most complete medical kit please? I need a stethoscope."

"Sure." Michelle looks around the room and finds one in the biggest medical kit bags.

Raphael listens to André's chest with a stethoscope. And then he freezes. He stares at André with an unreadable expression. André also stares back at Raphael with an unreadable expression.

"Thanks Raphael. I think I am fine now." André gets up and puts back his sweater and his jacket before Raphael can stop him.

Gaby cannot help but notice that Raphael and André act strangely.

"Can somebody tell me what happened? André is not seriously injured right?" Gaby asks worriedly.

"No. I feel much better now," André replies. Raphael seems to be back from his trance now.

"Yeah. I think it's fine. Your ribs are going to be bruised in the next few days. But you can put an ice pack to minimize the pain. Let me know if it gets worse, okay?"

"Yes. Thanks Raphael. Let's go back now. We have a plane to catch tomorrow morning," André says.

They return to the base and return their ski equipment. Gaby is still worried about André. So, she approaches him, "André, are you sure you are okay?" She asks with worry.

"Yes." André smiles.

"Is it true that that guy was going to hit me if you did not throw yourself into him?"

"It looked like he lost control of his skis. I was afraid that he may have crashed into you, so I jumped in without thinking. It wasn't your fault Gaby," André says. Gaby cannot help but feel guilty. André saved her. She was the one who was supposed to get hit but he protected her.

André must see guilt on Gaby's face. "Hey, do not ever blame yourself. It was me who made that decision. And it was the right decision. You are unharmed and I only got bruised. No broken ribs nor broken arms. I can still perform the concert."

"But you were just risking your life. It was a very steep slope. Why did you do that?"

"As I said, it was a reflex. And I didn't want you to get hurt."

"Please don't do something like that again next time."

"Sorry I can't. I would still make the same decision if it happened again," André grins. Gaby does not know what to say. She looks at André with disagreement.

"Weren't you going to do what I did if you were in my position?" André asks.

Gaby cannot answer. Of course the answer is yes.

Chapter 25

Sunday Evening
Beau Rivage

Raphael is still busy in his own thoughts after what happened at the ski resort. He does not like what he heard when examining André. André did not have broken ribs, thankfully. But he may have something more serious. He did not say anything back there because he was still not sure if he heard it correctly. Even though Raphael has not finished his residency, he has undergone five years of medical training since he was a third year medical student. Based on what he learned, he knows that something is not right. He needs to speak with André privately. He cannot let this slide.

He knocks at André's suite while Gaby and Michelle are upstairs in the bedroom, and Guillaume appears.

"Hey Raphael, what's up?"

"Can I come in?"

"Of course."

When he enters the suite, André is sitting on the couch with his laptop, working.

André raises his head from his laptop. "Hi Raphael. What's up?"

Raphael does not say anything right away. He is trying to find the right words. It is not his business to ask André about his personal health as he is not André's primary care physician. But what if he is not aware that he is in serious trouble? Raphael takes a seat on the couch. Guillaume also takes a seat beside André.

Raphael is unsure if he wants to talk to André while Guillaume is there, but it seems that they are very close like brothers. From what Gaby told him, André does not have any immediate family members left.

"I am sorry if I sound nosy, but, André, have you ever been diagnosed with a heart problem?"

André does not reply at first. He and Guillaume exchange glances.

"A heart problem like what?" André asks.

"When I examined you earlier, I heard a loud systolic murmur. It looks like you may have an aortic valve stenosis." Raphael tries to sound professional by inserting some medical jargon. "In case you were not aware," Raphael adds. Aortic valve stenosis is a condition where the aortic valve, which pumps blood from the heart to the rest of the body, is narrowing. If the valve is too narrow, the heart cannot pump the oxygen-rich blood to the rest of the body. Over time it may result in complications like heart failure.

"I was diagnosed with a bicuspid aortic valve at birth, but the doctor told me it is not serious if I am asymptomatic."

"Are you asymptomatic though? Based on what I heard, it seems like you have a pretty severe stenosis. And what you told me makes sense because a bicuspid aortic valve usually causes aortic stenosis," Raphael says. Although this usually happens in much older adults, like 50-60 years old, instead of 29.

"Do you often feel dizzy, light-headed, fatigued, chest pain, palpitation, and shortness of breath these days?" Raphael continues.

"I do. But I thought that was quite normal. I thought I am just more tired than usual because of the tour."

"In your case, it may be the signs that your condition has worsened."

Raphael returns to his suite. He does not know how to describe what he is feeling right now. He barely knows André but after three times listening to his extraordinary performances, and based on today at the ski resort, how André was willing to risk his life for Gaby, he realizes that he has also developed affection towards André just like Gaby and Michelle. He can see that André often made sacrifices for Gaby. He truly cares about her. So, now Raphael does not know what to do.

He glances at the baby grand piano in the corner. He notices that André and Gaby always pour their emotions into the piano. For the first time in his life, he regrets that he never took piano lessons seriously. He wants to release his emotions now but he does not know how. He cannot play hockey or tennis or squash as he usually does when he wants to release stress.

He sits on the piano bench and starts to press any keys randomly. He tries to make a melody based on some popular songs that he knows, but unfortunately, he has no musical talent whatsoever.

"Raphael? Is that you?" Gaby appears on the stairs. She is in her pajamas ready to sleep.

"Hi Gabs. Can you teach me how to play piano?"

"Since when are you interested in piano? You always think that it is boring." Gaby climbs down the stairs and sits on the piano bench beside Raphael.

"Not after listening to you and André's performances."

Gaby notices that her brother seems different than usual. He has been surprisingly quiet since they left the ski resort. And now he wants to play piano.

"Raphael, what happened?" Gaby asks.

"Nothing. I am just being melancholic right now." Raphael continues to press random keys on the piano.

"Is there something wrong with André?" Gaby asks.

"I hope not. Thankfully he is not badly injured."

"What is it then? Your face did not look good after examining him earlier today."

"I was just worried that he had broken ribs and pneumothorax. I saw him hitting the ground very hard and then that skier fell on top of him. He was very lucky today."

"I know. That made me feel really bad."

"Don't be. I am sure he would regret it more if it was you who got hit."

"You sound like you know him really well. Are you guys buddies now?"

"Not really. I have just started to see why you and Michelle admire him so much. He performed really well and I like the fact that he is protective towards you. How are you and him?"

Gaby blushes. She has not told either Raphael or Michelle about their kiss yesterday. She decides that this is the right time to tell Raphael.

"What? You guys already kissed?" Raphael is surprised. Gaby nods shyly.

"So you really like him then?"

"I do. I never felt this strong feeling towards any other guys," Gaby admits.

Deep inside, Raphael is even more worried. It seems that Gaby has fallen in love with André, and vice versa. What if Gaby finds out about André's condition? She will be extremely sad.

Raphael notices that Gaby looks very happy. Raphael has never seen his sister like this before. From that moment on, Raphael promises himself to do whatever he can to protect his sister's feelings.

Chapter 26

Monday Morning
Beau Rivage

André grabs an ice pack from the fridge and applies it against his ribs beneath his shirt. The bruises have started to appear but are still faint. It hurts a little bit if he takes a deep breath. But the pain is nothing compared to his worsening symptoms due to his heart problem. He did not expect that Raphael would find out about his condition just through a quick examination. He is impressed with Raphael's medical knowledge. And he knows Raphael is right. André can feel that he is getting weaker and more tired every day.

One more concert and six more days. After that he is done. He reminds himself.

André is excited about the concert in New York. He cannot wait to present Gaby to perform in front of the New York Philharmonic Orchestra. Gaby has made huge progress within these past two weeks. Both in terms of technique and musical interpretation. This will be a good opportunity for her. He also wants to spend more time with her in New York. Now he has a lighter workload as he has finished reviewing everything he needs to review for Gauthier Capital. He is satisfied with the valuation for the IPO. Gauthier Capital has invested a lot of money in this client. But the offer price to the public is triple their purchase price. He is very sure that they will be able to find buyers. Therefore, once he arrives in New York, he can focus on his Piano Concertos and focus on preparing Gaby for her next performance. Hopefully, they can spend more time together too.

He still remembers their kiss two days ago. He has never felt something like that before. She is very special and he feels something special with their kiss. With Gaby, he does not have to say much but it looks like they understand each other. He is relieved that Gaby was left unharmed after the accident at the Grand Massif yesterday. He cannot imagine how he would feel if something bad happened to Gaby. He can feel that Gaby feels the same towards him. She may feel terrible if something bad happens to him. She already looked worried yesterday just because of his minor injury. What if something bad happens to him? Is she going to be okay? André is sure she is. She is a tough girl. He smiles to himself.

"Hey, how are you feeling?" Guillaume asks. He has just woken up.

"Good, thanks."

"How are your ribs?" Guillaume notices that André is applying an ice pack to his side.

"Not bad. The bruises are starting to appear though."

"At least your hands and arms are fine."

"Yeah."

"I was surprised when you made that heroic act. That was very brave. But a minor injury is worth it for Gaby, eh?" Guillaume teases him.

"I might do the same to you," André says, laughing. "Oh, by the way, how is it going with you and Michelle? I saw an obvious attraction between the two of you."

Guillaume only laughs. "Not as intense as you and Gaby obviously. Michelle and I are just starting to become friends."

"Shall we just move to Toronto then after my concert finishes?" André asks.

Guillaume does not reply at first. He is looking at André closely. "Yes André. We can do everything you want after the concert. So make sure you stay healthy until the end."

*

Monday Morning
Geneva Airport

André, Gaby, Guillaume, Raphael, and Michelle are now waiting to board their plane to New York. André and Guillaume's flight will leave thirty minutes earlier than Gaby, Raphael, and Michelle's flight. New York is their last stop and they are excited. By now, they have been on the tour for three weeks. They left in early December and now it is almost Christmas. With Christmas just a few days away, the airport has put up some Christmas decorations.

André and Gaby are no longer being shy in expressing their attractions towards each other in front of Guillaume, Raphael, and Michelle. Everybody can see that André and Gaby are like an inseparable couple even though they have not made it official.

"How are your ribs?" Gaby asks when they sit in the waiting area by the giant window. They enjoy looking at several planes taking off and landing in front of them.

"It does not hurt as long as I don't bump into something."

"I see."

"Ready for the concert in New York?"

"I don't know. The piece I will be playing is the hardest so far. What if I screw up?" Gaby asks.

"You won't. I trust you."

"I started recording myself last week. When I heard it, it sounded so bad!"

"You recorded yourself? Can you show it to me?" André's face lightens up.

Gaby feels like she should not have said anything. She read somewhere that one way to improve your performance is to record yourself playing and watch it. That way you will be able to find your strengths and weaknesses and learn from them. But, showing her video to André is very embarrassing! He is a world class pianist!

André can feel Gaby's hesitation. "It's only me."

"Well, you are the problem. I don't mind showing this to Raphael, Michelle, or Guillaume, but you are the last person I want to show this to."

"Why? Because I am a pianist?" André laughs. Gaby does not know if she can get used to his perfect look. Especially when he is laughing. He is very handsome!

"Yes."

"Don't think of me as a pianist, then. Think of me as your piano teacher. Are you still embarrassed to show it if it is to your teacher?"

"Well..."

"I have seen you played many times. There is nothing to be embarrassed about. Only something to be proud of," André explains. Sometimes Gaby thinks that André hypnotizes her. First with his good looks and now with his smooth talk.

"Okay." Gaby takes out her phone from her pocket and scrolls through her videos. When she finds it, she gives her phone to André. André takes it and listens with his earphone. Gaby does not want to look at André's expression when watching her video. She was playing the Aeolian Harp, the piece she will be playing in New York.

André puts off his earphones when he finishes listening. "Okay. This is good. The melody is clear and you have a good technique for this. But in the middle part, it seems like you played the arpeggios a bit too loud so it distracted from the main melody. Also your tempo was a bit rushed towards the end. Otherwise, this is really good. Thank you for showing me this." This is what Gaby likes about André. He always gives constructive and honest feedback without sounding discouraging. He always says the positive things first, and then areas of improvement, and then positive again. Gaby knows some other great piano players who think very highly of themselves and always criticize other people's performances in a hurtful way. But André is very different. He is much better than the average pianist, but he is still very humble, polite, and respectful.

"Thank you. I appreciate that."

"Keep recording yourself. I also do that. I agree with you, when we first listen back, it may sound bad and embarrassing. But that's how we learn. Otherwise, you would never improve and just be satisfied with the status quo."

"True. I was surprised that when we listen to our own playing during live performance, it is very different from when we listen to ourselves in the video."

"That's because when we are in the middle of playing, we have to concentrate on our technique, fingers, emotion, etc. But when we are just watching, we focus only on the sound and ourselves in the video. I sometimes only listen to the sound recording without the video. To be more focused on the music itself."

"Oh I see. Thanks for your advice. That is super helpful."

"Anytime," André says.

There is a boarding announcement for André's flight. "Let's go back to Raphael and Michelle." André and Gaby rise from their seats, but André suddenly loses his balance. Gaby grabs both his arms reflexively, to prevent him from falling.

"Hey are you okay?" Gaby asks worriedly. She helps him steady himself.

"Oh yes. I am okay," André says after finding his balance again. He closes his eyes for a second. For a second, he seems like he is going to faint.

"Are you sure? Gaby notices that his face looks paler and he breathes faster now.

"I am just dizzy, because I stood up too quickly," André replies.

His explanation doesn't satisfy her. "Tell me if something is wrong okay?"

"Yes. Thank you. Let's go."

Chapter 27

Monday Evening
New York

When they land at John F. Kennedy airport, Gaby feels at home. They are back on the American Continent.

After they get their luggage, they meet André and Guillaume in the arrival hall. Then, they take two cabs to downtown Manhattan. They will be staying at The Plaza on Fifth Avenue. Gaby is enjoying the cab ride from JFK to Manhattan. She has been to New York several times but she is never bored travelling to New York. It is a huge city with a lot of places and things to explore.

The cab passes the Queensboro Bridge towards downtown Manhattan. It is seven at night and in New York, it is still rush hour. So, their cab is stuck on the Queensboro Bridge for a while. Gaby enjoys the night view of Manhattan skyline. It is very pretty. The lights from the cars stuck in the traffic make the city even prettier at night.

Finally their cabs arrive at The Plaza and they check in to the hotel. Because they are very tired after a long flight, they decide to just have dinner at The Palm Court, the restaurant inside The Plaza. Gaby has never been to this restaurant before. The restaurant is called The Palm Court because there are many tall palm trees inside the restaurant. The interior was designed to feel like they are eating in a luxurious indoor garden with a bright glass dome.

"So, what is our plan for tomorrow?" Guillaume asks after they ordered the food.

"I want to explore New Jersey. I have been to New York a thousand times, but I never explored the New Jersey area," Michelle says.

"Good idea. I am in."

"Gaby and I will be practicing the whole day. Right Gaby?" André looks at Gaby meaningfully. Back in Geneva, Gaby did not have a chance to spend more time with André. But now, she wants to spend more time with him. Just the two of them.

"Yes," Gaby says.

"What about you, Raphael?" Guillaume asks. Raphael does not seem enthusiastic since they arrived in New York. Gaby is wondering what is wrong.

"I am not interested in New Jersey, Michelle. So, you can go there with Guillaume. I might just enjoy some 'me' time in Brooklyn," Raphael says.

"Wait what? That does not sound like you at all, Raphael." Michelle looks confused.

"What do you mean? Of course I need alone time, too. Everybody does," Raphael replies.

"Well, how about just let us know if you change your mind. And then you can join us in Jersey," Michelle says.

"I won't, but thanks. Don't worry about me. Even though I am the one without a partner here, I am not lonely." Raphael shrugs.

"Why don't you find yourself one? C'mon, this is New York," Guillaume suggests.

"I am okay."

They continue to chat and eat until nine. After that, they go to the suite. This time they book two suites on a separate floor. Gaby, Raphael, and Michelle's suite is the Carnegie Two Bedroom Suite on the 19th floor overlooking Central Park. André and Guillaume's suite is the one bedroom Penthouse suite on the 20th floor with courtyard and skyline view. Originally, André and Guillaume only booked the Carnegie suite. But now they book the Penthouse suite and give up the Carnegie suite for Raphael, Gaby, and Michelle. What Gaby does not understand is, why André and Guillaume only book the penthouse with one bedroom? They don't sleep together, do they?

While waiting for the elevator, André and Guillaume's plan becomes obvious.

"Gaby, would you mind if I sleep at Carnegie tonight? You can have the penthouse," Guillaume says. At first Gaby does not realize what this means. Wait, does that mean?

She quickly looks at André. He is grinning. "If you want to sleep with Raphael and Michelle, that is fine too." She doesn't know how to respond. She looks at Michelle, "Michelle, you are okay with this?"

"A hundred percent." Michelle also grins.

"Raphael?"

"I'm cool with it. At least I have a bedroom for myself this time."

"And I need to take a break from André," Guillaume jokes.

"I also need to take a break from Guillaume," André says.

"Okay then," Gaby finally agrees.

"And both Carnegie and the Penthouse suites have a piano. So, tomorrow you can practice from Carnegie, I can practice from the penthouse," André explains.

"Sounds good to me," Gaby says.

Then the elevator stops at the 19th floor and then Guillaume, Michelle, and Raphael come out. They say good night to each other.

Now it is only André and Gaby. Gaby cannot help but feel nervous. So, are they going to sleep together in the same bedroom tonight?

They arrive in front of the penthouse suite. André swipes the key and they enter the suite. Wow. It is such a beautiful suite. The suite consists of two floors. The first floor consists of the living room with a baby grand piano, a study room, and a bathroom. Then, they climb an elegant staircase leading to the second floor. The second floor consists of a bedroom and there is a terrace! Gaby has never been to a suite like this before. She is wondering how much this suite costs per night.

Their luggage is already delivered to the bedroom. So, André and Guillaume have planned this apparently. Because it is Gaby's luggage instead of Guillaume's in the corner of the bedroom.

Gaby is not sure what to do next. What does André expect?

Gaby has never had any intimate relationship with anyone before. If she and André are going to do it tonight, it will be her first time. Is she ready to lose her virginity? There is no doubt that she loves André. However, losing her virginity is not something trivial for her. She would need some time to think and to be sure that she is ready and this is what she wants. And she does not think that this can be decided in less than an hour like this. Rather than doing it when she was not ready, she would rather wait. But how about André? Would he be disappointed if she does not want to do it tonight?

"Do you want me to show you?" André says suddenly.

"Show me what?" Gaby is tensed up.

"The Aeolian Harp?"

"Oh yes! Absolutely!" Gaby is relieved.

"Let's go downstairs."

They go downstairs to the piano in the living room. André sits on the bench and Gaby is standing next to him. Then he starts playing.

Wow. He plays it effortlessly. The music is flowing beautifully in his hands. The melody is very clear and he does the rubato perfectly. It sounds very different than when Gaby played it.

When he is done, Gaby is just speechless.

"Does it make sense?" André asks.

"Yeah, but I don't think I have the skills to play like you," Gaby says without confidence.

"Please take a seat here. How about play it slowly at first, but still pay attention and give emphasis to the melody," André says.

Gaby does what André says. She focuses on the melody while playing it slowly. It is not easy. She keeps experimenting with the touch. Sometimes she presses too hard, sometimes too soft. She needs to find the balance.

"Now, play it at the actual tempo."

Again, Gaby does what André says. And surprisingly, it seems like the melody flows better and sounds better now. Just like that!

"See? You are making progress!" André comments after Gaby finishes the piece. Gaby cannot help but feel excited. "You are right! Thanks!"

The room is dimly lit. The atmosphere is like a romantic candle light dinner, except that it is not a dinner but a piano lesson.

Gaby is affected by the music and the atmosphere. She kisses André on the cheek and says, "Thank you."

André seems surprised but genuinely happy. "No problem." He looks at Gaby in the eyes. They stare at each other for a while. And then

André starts to move his face closer to Gaby's. His hands are on Gaby's shoulders.

He kisses her on the lips.

It is the second time they kiss. André smells really good. The kiss is very gentle and tender. Gaby never felt like this before. Gaby kisses him back passionately. She puts her arms around André's neck. André puts his arms around her waist and now their bodies press against each other.

They forget where they are and they pour their feelings into each other. They breathe faster and become more and more passionate with each other. André's hands are now caressing her back intimately, and he starts to put his hand inside her blouse. Gaby wants to feel André more. She touches his chest and abs and then his side.

"Ouch," André groans. Gaby realizes that she is pressing his bruised side.

"Sorry!" Gaby says.

"That's okay," André says and then they continue kissing and touching each other. Gaby is more careful this time, but she is not sure how big the bruises are. So she starts unbuttoning his white shirt while they continue kissing. Oh my God, Gaby has never felt like this before. She wants him so badly. Finally she finishes unbuttoning his shirt and touches his skin directly. His skin is warm and smooth. He is very lean and muscular.

André lifts up Gaby's blouse and releases it from her head and arms. Gaby is only wearing a thin tank top under the blouse. André's hands are touching her bare shoulders and arms. She feels warm under his touch.

Then Gaby frees André from his shirt. She cannot believe that she is undressing André Gauthier-Lee, the pianist that she has admired forever. He is her long-life idol and now here he is shirtless in front of her. This is the third time he is half-naked in front of her, but this is the first time she touches his body. She releases her lips from him and takes a look at his body. It is hard not to notice his bruised side. It has turned blue. The bruise starts from his lower right chest and continues down to the tenth rib. His shoulder is also bruised. Apparently the accident at the ski resort the other day seemed to have damaged his body pretty badly. Now Gaby knows why he groaned in pain when she touched his side.

"This does not look good. It's because of me," Gaby says.

"No, it's not." André starts to kiss Gaby again. Gaby tries to distract herself away from his bruised body by kissing him. She is more careful not to touch his right side this time.

"Let's go to the bedroom," André says. They keep kissing and touching each other passionately while climbing the stairs until they get into the bedroom.

Once they get into the bedroom, André unbuttons her jeans and rolls down her jeans to her feet. Gaby freezes for a second. She has never felt this naked in front of anyone before. André senses her uneasiness.

"Is this your first time?" André looks up to Gaby. He is still kneeling down.

"Yes." Gaby hesitates.

"Let's just do what you are comfortable with then." He starts to kiss her again. Now Gaby is only wearing her tank top and panties. She feels very vulnerable in front of André, but she kisses him back. He puts her on the bed and he positions himself on top of her. Her arms are against his chest and she can feel that his heart is beating fast.

Then, André starts breathing hard and irregularly. It seems like he is panting and gasping for air. He withdraws his lips from her and backs off. Gaby is not sure what happened.

"Hey are you okay?" Gaby asks worriedly. André is still trying to catch his breath. His chest is moving up and down rapidly.

André does not answer and instead, he starts coughing. Gaby is panicking. She does not know what to do so she pats his back gently.

"I'm okay," André says after he finishes coughing. He puts his hand on his side again to guard his ribs. His breathing is still shallow and rapid.

"Is it because of your ribs?" Gaby starts to feel guilty. Didn't Raphael tell her that he does not have any broken ribs?

"No, it's not because of my ribs. Don't worry. Let's just go to sleep tonight. I'm sorry," André says. His face looks tired and a bit pale now.

"Are you sure you are okay? Should I call Raphael?"

"No. Please don't. I just had a mild asthma attack. It's not a big deal," André replies.

"Okay," Gaby says.

André walks towards the other side of the bed and starts to unbutton his jeans but then he stops and looks at Gaby. "Do you mind? I usually sleep only with..." André is too embarrassed to finish his sentence.

"I don't mind." Gaby blushes. Then André takes off his pants, leaving him only with his black Calvin Klein underwear. His legs are lean and strong too. He looks like a Calvin Klein model instead of a pianist.

They sleep side by side. Gaby notices that André puts two pillows behind his head. His breathing has slowed down but is still shallow. His chest is still up and down rapidly. It's like he has just finished running.

Gaby moves closer to him and lies her head on his left chest that is not bruised. She can hear his heartbeat is not as fast as before but it still sounds irregular. What's wrong with him? She puts her arms around his waist to hug him. Their bare legs also cross each other.

"Tell me if you don't feel well, okay?" Gaby says.

André nods and puts his arm around Gaby. He feels so much better and calmer when Gaby is in his embrace. They fall asleep in that position.

Chapter 28

Tuesday Morning
The Plaza

When Gaby wakes up that morning, André is no longer in the bed. But she knows where he is right away because she can hear the piano downstairs. André is playing E-minor scales.

Gaby quickly gets dressed and goes downstairs. She sees André behind the piano. He has showered and dressed in his usual white shirt and jeans.

"Morning, Gaby." André stops playing.

"Morning. How are you?" Gaby asks awkwardly. Last night was the first time they slept together. Even though nothing happened.

"I am good. How are you?"

"I'm good, thanks."

"Let's have some breakfast." André rises and walks to the dining table. Gaby follows him and sits in front of him. She grabs coffee and some bread.

"Did you sleep well last night?" André starts. Gaby blushes. It was the best night ever in her life. Even though they only kissed and hugged. Gaby felt very comfortable sleeping in his arms. She never felt that close to any man.

"Yes. Did you?"

"Yes. I did."

"What time did you wake up this morning?"

"Around six. Did my piano wake you up? I am sorry. Morning is the best time for me to warm up."

"Oh no, don't worry. I did not wake up because of your piano." Gaby bites her bread. She looks at André. Why does he maintain formality after the progress they made last night?

"So, are you going to practice again today?" André asks.

"Yes. I will practice in the suite downstairs. I won't bug you unless necessary." Gaby smiles.

"You can bug me anytime." He replies with a smile too and then he drinks his orange juice. "Do you want to go somewhere after practice?"

Gaby cannot hide her enthusiasm. "Where?"

"I was thinking about going skating at Rockefeller Center if you are up to it."

"Yeah, that sounds fun! I am in."

"Great. Text me when you are done practicing. I'll come and get you in your suite."

"Perfect."

After Gaby finishes showering, she goes down to the Carnegie suite on the 19th floor where Raphael, Michelle, and Guillaume sleep. She has the swipe key but prefers to knock.

Raphael opens the door. He looks like he has just woken up. His hair is still messy. "Hi Gabs. C'mon in." Gaby enters and looks around the suite. It is gorgeous as well. She can see the beautiful Central Park in the morning from the window in the living room.

"Have Guillaume and Michelle left?"

"Yes. They left early in the morning," Raphael says.

They sit in the living room. Gaby can see the exact same piano as in André's suite. Since there are only two of them in the room, Gaby feels like she wants to talk to Raphael. Raphael seems to read her mind.

"Is everything okay? How was last night with André?" Raphael asks, more worried than nosy.

Gaby doesn't know how to explain. "It was good. I mean, we practiced piano together and then we kissed and hugged, but we didn't do it. You know what I mean."

Gaby knows that other people may feel awkward talking about their sex life with their brother, but Gaby and Raphael are different. They are very close to each other. Gaby does not hesitate to talk to him.

"Why is that? Is it you or him or both who decided not to do it?" Raphael asks.

"It's a bit complicated. He knows I have never done it before. I kind of hesitated a little bit. Although, if he would have kept going yesterday, I would probably have let him. But then..." Gaby hesitates to continue.

"But what?"

"But he was suddenly running out of breath and started coughing. Then he looked very tired so we just went to the bed after and we did not do it. Is he okay, Raphael?"

"Coughing?"

"Yes."

Raphael does not reply at first. He is still thinking hard. Probably making a diagnosis.

"Why don't you check up on him again? What if he is sick because of that accident in the Alps? His side does not look good at all. The bruise is large. I feel so guilty," Gaby continues.

"The thing is, I prefer not to provide continuing care to family members or friends. And he is in a relationship with you. Do you think he is going to open up to me just because I am your brother? Instead, he probably would withhold important information about his health from me to make you stop worrying. So it would be best if I don't get involved in his healthcare matters."

"But you examined him last time."

"That was because it was an emergency, and there was no other available physician beside me."

"Can you think of this as an emergency too?"

"Gaby, I know what you are thinking. But don't worry. The bruise does not cause him to be out of breath or coughing."

"What is it then?"

"You have to ask him."

"You are not helpful. I am just worried."

"Don't worry. I can talk to him later, providing that he is willing to talk to me about his health problems. I can recommend some good doctors too if needed. So it all really depends on him. But if it is an emergency case, I will do everything I can to help."

"Okay. Thanks Raphael." Gaby feels slightly better. And then she starts practicing.

*

Raphael knocks at André's suite. He was going to go to Brooklyn today, but what Gaby told him this morning is distracting him. So, he decides to stop by to visit André.

André opens the door. He looks confused when he finds Raphael there.

"Raphael? Isn't Gaby downstairs with you?" André asks.

"Yes she is. But I want to talk to you. Can I come in?"

"Of course." André lets him in. They sit on the couch in the living room. Raphael does not know where to start. He does not want to ask about André's health if he is not willing to share that information with him.

"Gaby says you were coughing and out of breath last night. I just want to make sure you are okay. Do you feel any discomfort somewhere?"

"Not really. I think I've started to get used to these symptoms by now." André replies.

"Are you aware that experiencing these symptoms more often could mean that your condition is progressing to heart failure?"

"Yes, that's what my doctor has warned me."

Every time he talks to André, he discovers more problems. Raphael realizes that André is not going to lie but he is not going to tell the truth voluntarily either. Raphael is wondering what else André is hiding. He has to throw all the possible worst-case scenarios until André reveals all the truths.

"Have you ever been diagnosed with any other heart problems related to your bicuspid aortic valve, like aortic aneurysm for example?" Raphael asks. Aortic aneurysm is a condition where the aorta is bulging like a balloon. It's one of the most common complications caused by bicuspid aortic valve. Over time the aortic aneurysm may dissect or rupture and the result will be fatal.

André looks surprised. It seems like he did not expect Raphael to know that.

André does not answer at first. So Raphael continues, "Listen André, you don't have to talk to me. I am not your family physician. I am talking to you now as a friend. Not as a doctor. Maybe I can help recommend some good cardiologists or cardiothoracic surgeons."

"Actually, you are right. That's what my doctor also told me a few months ago. He said that I have an aortic aneurysm too and I need a surgery."

Raphael feels his fears turn into reality. So, it is not only aortic stenosis, but also an aortic aneurysm. With aortic stenosis only, the surgery can be much simpler. He may be a good candidate for TAVR surgery (Transcatheter Aortic Valve Replacement), which is a less risky heart surgery without opening the chest. But with aortic aneurysm, it looks like he cannot avoid the open heart surgery. And if his doctor has recommended surgery, that means the aneurysm may have dilated significantly.

What Raphael doesn't understand is why André is still travelling around the world with this condition? He even went skiing and overexerted himself, which can be very dangerous for his condition.

"With severe aortic stenosis, heart failure, and aortic aneurysm, delaying your surgery is extremely risky. What if your aneurysm ruptures before the surgery? We are on a ticking time bomb right now."

"I know, that is why I planned this concert right after I received my diagnosis. In case these will be my last concerts."

Chapter 29

Tuesday Evening
Rockefeller Center

As usual, there is a huge Christmas tree in the middle of Rockefeller Center. Gaby and André are skating that evening. André is a better skater than Gaby, so most of the time she is holding his hand and André is always the one who pulls her towards him. They really enjoy the snow, the Christmas atmosphere, and of course each other's presence.

André looks really cool with a double breasted suit today. He is as elegant as always. Gaby herself tried to dress up better since they are going out together. She is wearing a long red coat and she put on light makeup. She feels like today is their first official date as they made plans to spend time together aside from practicing piano.

Gaby suddenly trips and falls backwards. André moves very fast and puts his right hand behind Gaby's head to prevent her head from hitting the ice. But because he is doing so, he falls on top of Gaby. He feels the pain again when his ribs bump into Gaby's. But at least Gaby's head is safe on his hand.

"Are you okay?" André asks Gaby.

"Yes, thank you! You have just saved me again." Gaby looks at him. His body is still on top of her. Their faces are almost touching each other. They look at each other for a few seconds. Then, suddenly, André kisses her very quickly on the lips and gets up. Wow, what is that?

"Sorry. I cannot help it." André grins mischievously. He offers his hand to help Gaby get up.

"Your ribs are still okay?" Gaby checks in after she is able to stand steadily.

"Yes. Do you want to rest for a bit?" André asks.

"Yes."

"Let's get off the ice."

They buy some hot chocolate. Gaby feels warmer now. André is standing beside her with a red cheek due to the cold air. They have been outside for about one and a half hours.

"I have something for you," André says.

"What is that?" Gaby asks curiously.

André pulls something from his pants' pocket. It is a beautiful silver pendant with a G key in five music lines. Gaby is amazed. She has never seen something that beautiful.

"Do you like it?"

"Yes. Very much." Gaby touches the pendant on his hand.

"Let me put it on you." André smiles. Gaby turns her body so that her back is facing André. Then, he puts the pendant around her neck. After that, she turns to face him.

"Thank you so much! I really appreciate it." Gaby touches the pendant on her neck again.

"My pleasure."

"Let me buy you something next time," Gaby says.

André laughs. "Don't worry. Just play piano more often for me. It is enough to make me happy."

"I am wondering, what if I cannot play piano? Do you think we would still be like this?"

"If you cannot play but your spirit was the same, then yes, I think I would still like you," André says. That is the first time Gaby hears that he likes her.

"I really admire your persistence when we practice. You know your strengths and weaknesses in playing piano and you always try to improve your weaknesses. You were hurt by other people's comments but you don't give up. You keep going." André continues.

"Thank you for your kind words."

"What about you? If I could not play piano, would you still like me? Assuming that you like me." André grins again.

"Of course I do like you. But, I have to be honest. I noticed your piano skills before your physical appearance or personality. But the more I get to know you, the more your piano skills do not matter anymore. You have an awesome personality. You always encourage and support other people. You are always selfless and taking risks for other people. I like spending time with you," Gaby says honestly.

André is speechless. No one has ever complimented him like Gaby just did. He feels good to be appreciated because of his personal qualities and not his piano skills.

He hugs her again. He never wants to let her go.

*

Tuesday Evening
Brooklyn

Raphael always enjoys walking along Brooklyn Bridge. He has just crossed from Manhattan to Brooklyn on foot via Brooklyn Bridge. He can see the New York skyline view at night better from Brooklyn.

Raphael is enjoying his "me" time at one of the Brooklyn Bridge Park Piers. This is the vacation he has been waiting for. Unfortunately, he is no longer in a vacation mode. Since he discovered André's condition, he has switched to a work mode again.

Since he was a medical school student, he has always taken ownership of all the cases assigned to him. He thinks about and analyzes the cases almost constantly. Whenever he does rounds in the morning, the attending physician is always impressed with his thorough understanding of each patient. It is like he memorizes all the information on the patient chart.

Now he is thinking about André just like he is thinking about his other patients. Even though André is not his patient, he still feels that he has a duty of care towards him. He feels responsible. Maybe because André is in a relationship with Gaby and they are all travelling together now.

There are five more days until the concert. What can possibly happen in five days? He plans to take André to the hospital right after his concert. They cannot wait any longer than five days. He has done his research and decided that Columbia University would be his first choice for André's surgery.

So, he has done everything he can right? So why is he still feeling uneasy? If something happens to André, he might blame himself. He understands now why a physician shouldn't treat family members or friends. But it's too late. He is already too involved now.

*

Tuesday Evening
New Jersey

Guillaume is walking along the Hudson River Waterfront Walkway with Michelle. They had a great day today exploring Jersey City such as visiting the 9/11 memorial empty sky and Newport Centre. Michelle is a great company. She is a bit chatty, easygoing, full of energy, and beautiful. Guillaume's love of classical music is equivalent to Michelle's love of classical ballet. As they spend time together more often, he learns more about ballet works, technique, and choreography. He always enjoyed watching ballet but was never able to distinguish good versus bad technique. And the only choreographer he knows is the famous George Balanchine.

Michelle may look superficial for someone who doesn't know her yet. However, Guillaume could see that she is very loyal and is always supportive towards Gaby. She is always ready when Gaby needs her. Moreover, she is also a very hardworking person. She strives in a competitive ballet world and managed to become a soloist with a major ballet company in Toronto. Although she is only 23 years old, Guillaume could see the mature side of her.

Sometimes Michelle also did a little practice in their suite. Guillaume couldn't take his eyes off her whenever she did the *arabesque* pose or *pirouette*. Listening to Michelle talking about ballet and watching her practicing are good distractions from his day-to-day routine.

Especially these days.

He really needs a distraction from André. He cannot stop thinking and worrying about his friend. Since André told him about his condition before they started the trip, he was in distress. He is not worried about losing a client. He can always find another client. But if he is going to lose a brother and a friend like André, he really cannot help it. And he knows that André's condition is getting worse every day. He can feel it too.

"Guillaume?" Michelle calls him back from his lamentation.

"Yes? Sorry. I was distracted. What did you say?" Guillaume feels guilty.

"It's not important. Are you okay? What are you thinking?"

"Oh nothing."

"C'mon Guillaume. What is it?"

"Oh, I am just worried about André. He is working too hard. I am worried that his health may be impacted."

"Oh, I see. Actually, I noticed it, too. He looked very tired and a bit depressed when he was not around Gaby. But when Gaby was around him, he looked fine to me."

"Well, he is in the middle of a big concert tour. No wonder if he is tired and stressed because of the pressure."

"Do you know why he is retiring? He is playing very well. What a waste."

"He has his reasons," Guillaume says.

"Don't worry. Gaby will take care of him. And vice versa. They look really great together, don't they?"

"Yes. I actually have never seen André like this before."

"Like what?"

"He used to be very strict, very disciplined, and would always do everything by himself. But now, he smiles and laughs more often. He is more relaxed as well. I am really glad that he met Gaby. He has found his match."

"So has Gaby. I can feel something different in her, too. In positive way. She seems to be more enthusiastic about life, more motivated, and more energetic. Oh, not to mention her piano performance. It has improved a lot since she learned from André. André has had a great impact in her life."

Not only in Gaby's life, but also in his, Guillaume thinks.

Chapter 30

Wednesday Morning
The Plaza - Central Park

As usual, by the time Gaby wakes up, she hears André warming up on the piano. What a morning person he is. Last night, they went to sleep right away because they were tired after skating. Gaby slept on André's chest again with his arms around her. She felt so secure and warm in his hug. Gaby is wondering why André did not take it forward to the next step, but to be honest, at this point she is comfortable with what they have been doing. Maybe André does not want to rush it either and she is fine with it. If it is the right thing to happen, she believes it will happen naturally.

André, Gaby, Guillaume, Raphael, and Michelle have agreed to a short morning run in Central Park. Gaby changes into her hoodie and training pants and she goes downstairs. She sees André behind the piano already wearing his training pants and long sleeves top for the run.

"Morning Gaby." André greets her politely and he stops playing.

"Morning."

"Did you sleep well last night?"

"Yes I did. How about you?"

"Yes. I sleep better these days. Thanks to you," André says.

"Me too."

"Are you ready? Let's go." They agree to meet Raphael, Guillaume, and Michelle in the lobby for the run today. They both go down the elevator to the lobby. They wait for less than five minutes before Raphael, Guillaume, and Michelle appear in their workout clothes.

"Morning guys!" Guillaume says excitedly.

"Morning. Ready?" Gaby says. He nods. So do Raphael and Michelle.

The five of them cross the 59th street to Central Park. Even though it is winter, the jogging trail in Central Park has been cleared of snow. The snow is piled up on both sides of the trail, but they are still careful in case the trail is slippery. They start warming up by walking faster. Then, they increase their speed to a jog. Eventually, they start to run.

Gaby notices that Raphael always runs beside André. They seem to have a serious conversation throughout the run.

"Are you doing okay, André? Don't push yourself if you feel tired," Raphael says.

"So far, so good," André says.

However, the track starts to go uphill. André can make it to the top of the hill even though he is the last. But by the time he arrives at the top, he is panting again. His face becomes pale and he starts coughing.

"Okay, let's take a break guys," Raphael says. He offers his water bottle to André.

Gaby is confused. The hill is not that high and the incline is not that steep. Why is André so out of breath? Someone who is physically fit like him should be able to climb to the hilltop easily?

"Are you okay, André?" Gaby asks.

"Yes." He is still out of breath.

"What's wrong?" Michelle approaches them and looks at André.

"Nothing. I am just not as fit as I thought," André replies.

Guillaume gives him a concerned look. "I think we should stop now."

"You guys can continue. Don't worry about me. I am going to take a break for a sec," André says.

"Let's just stick together," Gaby says.

They wait until André can catch his breath. Gaby is pretty sure that there must be something wrong with him. These incidents happen too often to be just regular fatigue. She remembers he almost fell when they were in the airport in Geneva. And when they almost had sex the other day, he couldn't continue because he was running out of breath.

"Is it your asthma again?" Gaby asks.

"Kind of," André says.

Then, after André is able to catch his breath, they continue to run slower. Luckily, they don't have to climb the hill again.

At ten, they finish running and go back to their suite. Gaby showers in the bathroom on the top floor while André showers in the bathroom next to the study room. By the time Gaby finishes, André is already in front of the piano. His hair is still wet. So is Gaby's. Gaby plans to practice again in the Carnegie suite today while André is practicing in the penthouse.

André looks up from his piano when she approaches him. "Ready to practice?" he asks.

"Yes," Gaby replies. "Are you feeling better now? I was worried when you were out of breath."

"I'm okay. Don't worry." Gaby's face does not seem satisfied with his answer. So, he continues, "There is something you don't know yet about me. Since I was a kid, I was always good at studying and piano, but I was never good at sports because I was always the weakest and the slowest in my class. Also, I got sick often when I was young. I know some girls like strong guys with big muscles."

"Really? But you are really good at skiing and skating. You seem very athletic and fit." Gaby tries not to think about his chest and six-pack when he was shirtless.

"Well, skiing and skating are just for fun, and they do not take a lot of energy if your technique is good. I appear athletic and fit because I used to swim a lot. But I don't anymore due to my workload."

"I see." Gaby still thinks something does not add up.

"Let's focus on our concert on Saturday. Don't worry about me." André smiles encouragingly. Gaby nods.

*

Wednesday Afternoon
The Plaza

André starts practicing his Piano Concerto No. 1 in E minor Op. 11. This is his favourite of all Chopin's pieces. It summarizes all of his feelings throughout the concert tour, from the start until now. He remembers he started the concert in Singapore with a lot of pressure from work as well as loneliness. But then he met Gaby and his life became brighter and livelier. In Geneva, he was swamped again with work and also with Charmaine and he did not spend much time with Gaby. He remembers those unpleasant and quiet lonely nights. In New York, he has made great progress with Gaby in terms of their relationship. They got closer physically and emotionally. However, while his relationship progressed, so did his heart condition. Deep down, he is quite frustrated that he can only do limited things to express his feelings towards Gaby. Every time they want to move forward with their relationship, his heart restricts him.

André has no choice but to wait. He will need to fix his heart condition before confessing his feelings to Gaby. He never had someone who understands him as much as her. He is very comfortable around her. He can show his vulnerability too because he feels safe with her. He wants to declare his love and make love with her. But in order to do that, he'll need to survive.

Chapter 31

Thursday
New York

Gaby and André decide to take a day off from practicing. They plan to explore New York City together.

Their first destination is the famous Statue of Liberty. This statue was given to the United States as a gift from France in 1886. This statue is a symbol of freedom and of welcome to the immigrants who arrived by the sea. They take a ferry from Battery Park to Liberty Island. Gaby is never bored visiting the Statue of Liberty and seeing the New York skyline from the Liberty Park. This time is even more special because she is with someone special. André also has been here multiple times but he looks like he is enjoying himself as well.

After the Statue of Liberty, they get on the ferry to continue to Ellis Island. They enter the National Museum of Immigration and explore the history of immigrants in America. On the second floor, they can see the registry room, where people had to undergo the immigration inspection during peak immigration years from 1890 - 1954. The inspection process included medical and mental examination. Therefore, only those who were healthy could be accepted into the new country. Gaby is glad that when her parents immigrated to Canada, it was very different from when these immigrants came to America. Her grandparents in Hong Kong sent her parents to Canada for a better education because they had money. But these immigrants came to America because of famine, poverty, and oppression in their countries of origin.

Because of this visit to Ellis Island, André himself is reminded of his Korean mother, who also immigrated to Montreal when she was a teenager. He tells Gaby about his deceased mother. His mother was a lovely and very nurturing mother, he says. She always supported him when he burned out from practicing. His dad, on the other hand, was more strict and encouraged discipline.

"Do you miss your mom?" Gaby asks.

"Yes. All the time."

"She must be very proud of you. Even from up there."

"Thank you."

Gaby also tells André more about her parents and her happy childhood memories. She really hopes that André can meet her parents after they finish the concert in New York.

After Ellis Island, they return to Manhattan and have lunch at the Brookfield Place's food hall. They eat and chat while enjoying the view of the Hudson River and New Jersey. After lunch they take a walk along the Battery Park City Esplanade. Whenever she visits a place with André, it is more beautiful than when she visited before.

"Why do you like Chopin so much?" Gaby asks.

"Because I feel like I can understand him. Chopin was actually a very sensitive person. His health was always frail as well. These facts reflected in the way he always tried to make every note very meaningful and delicate. Also, he was not very friendly and did not have many friends," André explains.

"I feel like you are very different from Chopin. You are very friendly and warm."

"Really? You think so?" André asks in surprise. "I am not good at making friends. You see, Guillaume is my only friend. I never had close friends before because I am naturally very introverted."

"I think many people want to be friends with you, because you are naturally a good person. You always push people to be the best version of themselves. But I do agree with you being an introvert. You seem to have your own world. So you kind of keep your distance from other people. There is nothing wrong with that."

"Do you feel you are outside of my world?" André asks.

"Sometimes," Gaby admits.

"How so?"

"I feel like you are kind of keeping me on edge right now. But you never really let me into your life," Gaby says. André seems to digest what Gaby says.

"Are you disappointed?"

"No. If there are certain things you are not comfortable discussing with me, I am not going to push you. Take your time. We have only known each other for a few weeks."

"Thanks, Gaby. It is not that I don't trust you. You and Guillaume are the closest people to me now. But I let time be the one to guide me. Sorry if I come across distant."

"Oh no, don't be sorry. Keep being who you are. I like the way you are." Gaby smiles.

"I like the way you are too," André says and grabs her hand.

After they enjoy walking along the pier, they cross the West Street to stop by the 9/11 memorial. Even though both of them knew no one who was affected by the 9/11 attack, they bow their heads and have a moment of silence for the 9/11 victims. Gaby is sad to see the two holes on the ground. They used to be the tall twin towers.

It's already six, so they take the subway from Park Place to 34 St – Penn station to go to Midtown Manhattan. It's been a while since André rode public transport. He usually goes everywhere by cab. But it is the second time he rides the subway that day. The first time was this morning when they rode the subway from The Plaza to Battery Park. He does not mind doing anything he is not used to as long as he is doing it with Gaby. Every activity done together with Gaby becomes more fun for him.

They decide to eat dinner at one of the Korean restaurants in Koreatown. Gaby really likes Korean food and so does André. He always preserves his own Korean roots. Gaby is even more surprised when he orders the food in Korean. This is the first time Gaby hears André speak another language besides English or French. André speaks like a native Korean. Gaby is not even sure that she can speak Cantonese as well as a native of Hong Kong.

"Wow, that was amazing. Is Korean also your first language?" Gaby is impressed.

"French would be my first language. My English and my Korean are at the same fluency level. I used to speak Korean with my mom all the time."

"I see. That is so cool." Gaby is very impressed. If André said that his Korean is as good as his English, then he is a trilingual. André speaks English almost perfectly, only sometimes there was a slight French accent and sometimes he didn't pronounce the h where it was supposed to be pronounced (for example, he pronounced *otel* instead of hotel).

"How about you? I know English must be your first language. But your French is pretty good too!"

"Yeah, English is my first. French is second, but sometimes I still make grammar mistakes with French and I can never hide my English accent. I can understand Cantonese, but I am not that fluent."

"That is still good. For someone who has never lived in Quebec, I am very impressed with your French, actually."

"That's because I went to a French immersion school. But again, you always excel in everything you do much more than me. In piano, finance, second and third languages, sports, and who knows what else. I am not jealous by the way. In fact, I am happy for you."

"Most of the things I can do well are due to hard work as well. I have always practiced piano for at least five hours a day since I was young. Even with piano lessons, my dad still pushed me to be the best student in school as well. So, I studied hard and did my school assignments at night until two in the morning. In Quebec, the majority of people are bilingual, so my bilingualism is not unique. When it comes to sports, I really suck. I spend my time playing piano and studying too much. I barely pay attention to my body. And as I told you, I used to be a sickly kid."

"How about now? Has your health improved?"

"I wish. When I was in university, I used to swim a lot. And then I did not get sick as often as before and I felt more energized. But now, there is not much time to exercise in the middle of the tour. So I can feel that I am not as strong as I used to be." André gives a diplomatic answer.

That still does not explain why he is always out of breath and cannot walk uphill. But Gaby decides not to push him further. If he does not want to talk about it, Gaby will give him some space.

"I can say the same thing about you. You are very talented at the piano. I am sure that you are also good at your accounting job. You speak three languages as well. And you have such an awesome personality: strong, honest, and caring."

"Thank you," Gaby blushes.

"Let's go. We have one last stop," André says after they finish their meals.

Their last stop is the Empire State Building. Another thing they have in common is that they really like to enjoy the city view from higher places. Especially the night city view.

So they enjoy it, as they kiss on the rooftop of the Empire State Building on Christmas Eve.

Chapter 32

Friday Afternoon
Carnegie Hall

It is a beautiful Christmas day and the snow is still thick on the ground. The Christmas decorations at every corner of the city infuse the gloomy winter with the holiday spirit.

André will start practicing with the New York Philharmonic Orchestra today. But before he does, he and Gaby arrive at Carnegie Hall to practice by themselves.

André lets Gaby practice first while he is listening from the audience. It's been a while since he enjoyed someone's performance from the audience. Even though Gaby will only play one Etude, he is still excited to watch her. She is very graceful behind the piano and her fingers are very skillful.

André really appreciates when Gaby tries to perfect every note that she plays. Even if she presses the right note, if it does not sound the way she wants it to, she will repeat that part until she is satisfied. André does the same thing all the time. It shows that she takes this seriously. She is a perfectionist just like him. Piano is not just for fun, but she dedicates herself to the music and tries to make it perfect so that the audience can enjoy the best.

For André, meeting Gaby during his concert tour is a blessing. Gaby helps him get to know himself and appreciate himself as well because she is very blunt when giving compliments and feedback. Many other girls always expect compliments and the best treatment for themselves. But Gaby never hesitates to be the one who gives compliments and shows appreciation. For him, she is one of a kind and very precious.

After Gaby is done with her practice, it is André's turn to practice. He walks up to the stage when Gaby walks down.

"Hey, would you mind waiting for me until all the orchestra members have arrived? After that you can either wait for me here or go back on your own. I will finish at around six," André explains. Carnegie Hall is only an eight-minute walk from The Plaza anyway.

"Yes, I will wait until I meet them. I would love to stay until you finish." Gaby smiles.

"Thanks." André gives her a quick kiss on the cheek. Then he walks to the piano and starts practicing. Gaby sits in the front row and watches him. She feels so privileged to be able to enjoy André's private rehearsal both in the hotel suite and on the stage when nobody is around. Both Piano Concertos No.1 and 2 are approximately forty minutes each. Gaby is very impressed that André has memorized the pieces very well. She cannot wait to watch him playing with the orchestra.

At three, all the orchestra members have arrived to practice. André quickly introduces Gaby to the conductor and the concertmaster. They look very professional and intimidating. She would lose her guts if she had to play with this professional orchestra. They look like people who cannot tolerate imperfection. But André seems as confident as them because he is ready with his pieces.

By the time they start practicing, Gaby is impressed with their professionalism and perfectionism. They warm up first, and then run down Piano Concerto No. 1. After they finish the rundown, they discuss where things can be improved and then play only that part. They do the same with Piano Concerto No. 2. This is by far the most arduous practice Gaby has ever seen. But again, André does his part very well as always. And the conductor is very pleased with him.

*

Friday Evening
The Plaza

André and Gaby finish their practice and go back to The Plaza. They have agreed to have dinner together with Guillaume, Michelle, and Raphael at The Rose Club. Guillaume, Michelle, and Raphael want to drink some cocktails on Christmas day. However, André and Gaby decide not to drink. They still want to practice again tomorrow morning so they do not want to get drunk.

"Are you guys ready for tomorrow?" Guillaume asks when they enjoy their dinner at the Rose Club. Gaby really enjoys the ambience at the Rose Club. The seat is very comfortable and the lighting and the music are very conducive for casual chat.

"Not really. There's so much pressure with the New York Philharmonic. Even though I won't be the one who plays with them," Gaby says.

"You are good, Gabs. Don't worry," André adds.

"What were you guys doing yesterday and today?" Gaby asks Guillaume, Michelle, and Raphael.

"Yesterday we went to the Lincoln Centre and Juilliard School. Only Guillaume and I though. Raphael did not want to come with us. And then last night we explored Times Square. And today we just chilled in the hotel," Michelle says.

"What have you been doing, Raphael?" André asks.

"I went sightseeing at Columbia University yesterday. Just to look around, you know. That was my number one choice when applying to Med School, but unfortunately, I did not get accepted seven years ago. Today I walked along 5th avenue. Nothing much. How about you two?"

Gaby recounts their itinerary since yesterday. She realizes that they visited quite a lot of places: the Statue of Liberty, Ellis Island, Brookfield Place, the 9/11 memorial, and the Empire State Building.

"Wow, that's a lot. And did you still practice six hours today? That's impressive. You must be tired," Michelle comments.

"Kind of. Tomorrow is our big day," Gaby says.

"Make sure you guys get a lot of rest today," Raphael says.

They continue to chat until ten and then decide to go back to their suites. When they are waiting for the elevator, Raphael pulls André aside, "Can we talk for a sec?" and he looks at Guillaume, Michelle, and Gaby, "You guys can go ahead first."

So André stays with Raphael while the three of them enter the elevator. Gaby gives them a curious look before the elevator door is closed.

"How are you feeling, André?" Raphael asks.

"Still surviving. I am fine. Thanks for asking," André says.

"I have scheduled a check-up this Sunday morning at Columbia University Hospital. The doctor has agreed to give a consultation and examination. You could also get MRA (Magnetic Resonance Angiography) on the same day. I am afraid we cannot wait until you go back to Montreal."

"Thanks Raphael. Sure, I can make it. Could you come with me as well?"

"Yes I can."

When André goes back to the penthouse suite, he finds Gaby in the middle of practicing. She seems a bit tired and tense. André sits on the couch beside the piano to listen. Gaby's piano is the best sound that can distract him from his chest pain. He started to have mild chest pain during the practice with the NYPO this afternoon. Luckily it was still bearable so he could continue to practice. At dinner, he tried not to think about his pain and focused on the conversation instead. Luckily no one noticed.

Suddenly Gaby stops in the middle of the piece. She puts her face on her hands.

"Gaby, what's wrong?" André asks worriedly.

"It seems that I cannot make this note right. I start to lose control of the tempo as well. It's less than twenty-four hours until the concert. What should I do?" Gaby raises her head from her hands and looks at him. Gaby looks like she is about to cry.

"That happens to me too when I am tired and over-practiced. You need some rest, Gaby. You can wake up earlier tomorrow and practice again." He rises from the couch and stands beside Gaby and caresses her head gently.

"I can't. I cannot sleep until I get this part right," Gaby says frantically.

"Gaby please, do not put pressure on yourself. You have done amazing this afternoon. Come here." André pulls Gaby towards him and gives her a hug. They have not hugged for a minute when Gaby frees herself from him and runs to the bathroom. André can hear her retching and throwing up.

'Oh no,' he thinks. He quickly follows Gaby to the bathroom. He finds her kneeling in front of the toilet.

"Don't come here, please," Gaby says. She flushes the toilet quickly before André can see that she threw up the food they ate in The Rose Club earlier.

"Are you okay?" André looks extremely worried now. He pats Gaby's back gently.

"Yes. This happens when I am stressed," Gaby says weakly.

"Let me get you to the bed okay? We really need to rest. If you practice again tonight, it would do more harm than good to you. When you are tired, you can make dumb mistakes and it will ruin your confidence for tomorrow," André says sympathetically. Gaby digests what he says, and his words make sense.

"Okay, I will rest." Gaby says.

They go upstairs and Gaby goes to the bathroom to brush her teeth and change her clothes. André waits for her outside uneasily. Is she okay inside?

Finally, Gaby exits the bathroom with a fresher face even though she still looks tense.

"Do you want to go to the balcony?" André asks. She nods. They pass the hallway and go out to the balcony. The view of the New York skyline is so cool. So many beautiful lights. They stay silent for a few minutes.

"Gaby, I am really sorry to put this pressure on you," André starts.

"No, don't be. This is the best thing that ever happened in my life. It is not your fault at all. You are the one I should thank. It is all me who has to deal with this situation."

"I know it's stressful. But I cannot help but to repeat this again and again. You are doing awesome. You know that we are very similar. I am a perfectionist too. So you should feel confident about yourself when a perfectionist compliments your performance," André says.

'He is right,' Gaby thinks.

"This also happened to me before. Especially in the beginning of my career. It's normal, Gabs. Everyone experiences this. Pressure, anxiety, and expectation. You already finished two concerts very well. Remember that."

"But this piece is the hardest. Gosh, what was I thinking when I chose this piece?"

"It's always good to challenge yourself. You will have to start performing some hard pieces eventually. And if you can pass this, then you gain experience on how to handle pieces like this in the future," André explains.

"You are right," Gaby says. She just has to face it.

They stare at the beautiful night for a while before going back to bed to sleep. Gaby sleeps on André's chest again and she feels calmer.

Chapter 33

Saturday Afternoon
The Plaza

Today is the big day for both André and Gaby. It is their last and biggest concert. However, the atmosphere that day does not look very good. Firstly, there is a big snowstorm that morning. Gaby is watching the snowstorm from her bedroom window at The Plaza. She is just hoping that the storm will calm down before their concert starts.

Secondly, today is the first time Gaby wakes up earlier than André. André says he is going to sleep a little bit more. It is very unusual as he usually wakes up early in the morning and starts warming up at six. Gaby warms up first that morning, and practices her piece several times until it runs smoothly. She hopes that her practice today will be different from last night. Thankfully, André was right. Playing piano when you are tired and burnt out can create a death spiral. When you are too tired, you start making dumb mistakes. Because you keep making mistakes, you become anxious. Because you are anxious, your hands tense up and you cannot control your speed. That was what happened to her yesterday. But today, she is fresh and more relaxed and she can play her piece smoothly with a controlled tempo.

At around eleven, André appears on the staircase. He looks more tired and paler than usual. He goes down the stairs carefully.

"Are you alright?" Gaby rises from the piano.

"Yes, I am fine. Just a bit tired," André says. Gaby touches his forehead. Luckily, he does not have a fever. Then why is he looking unwell?

"Are you not feeling well?"

"Yeah, a little bit. But I am okay. Thanks for asking."

"Let's eat breakfast." Gaby leads André to the dining table. She ordered breakfast earlier, but André had not woken up yet.

"Thanks for ordering this Gaby. It's my favourite." André points at his egg benedict.

"No problem." Gaby is still worried about him. "Are you sure you don't want to call Raphael to check up on you? Your face does not look good," Gaby continues.

"I am fine," André says. He notices that Gaby still looks unconvinced.

"This happens a lot during my concerts. That's why I never scheduled a world tour concert for more than a month."

"André, please don't push yourself like this. If you are not feeling well, you can just cancel the concert."

"I cannot, unfortunately. But don't worry, in less than twelve hours, we will be done with the concert. Aren't you excited?"

"Yeah." Gaby still sounds very worried.

"Today, I will give the best performance. Especially for the last piece, Piano Concerto No. 1. That is your favourite, right?" André asks.

Gaby is surprised. "How did you know?"

"Because that's my favourite too."

After breakfast, Gaby goes to the Carnegie suite to practice while André is practicing in the penthouse. André feels relieved that Gaby has not found out about his condition. He does not want her to worry about anything before tonight's performance. He is afraid that her performance will be affected if she knows his real condition.

This morning, he woke up with chest pain and palpitations again. He is glad that Raphael has booked an appointment for his check up tomorrow. He does not think he can bear the symptoms much longer. Before, he barely noticed his fatigue, chest pain, pounding heart, and dizziness. He thought that those were normal. But now they have become consistent and he is no longer able to ignore it. He knows that there is a possibility that he has to undergo a heart surgery tomorrow. But he does not want to think about it today. Today, he should just focus on his concert.

When he starts practicing, he temporarily forgets about his symptoms. He plays the Piano Concerto as best as he can. He wants the audience to feel what he feels through this beautiful Piano Concerto. Especially Gaby. He wants her to enjoy it. This is the best gift he can give her, as she has been willing to accompany him throughout the tour and even perform with him. For him, these concerts feel very different from other concerts that he had before. These concerts are more colorful, with more ups and downs, and more variety of emotions and expressions.

André finishes practice at around three. When he goes to shower, he looks at the bruises on his side, which have now turned to blue-greenish. He cannot help but to think about Gaby. If he is not around, can she take care of herself? But he will survive to be together with her and protect her, won't he? There is a possibility that today could be his last day on earth. He promises himself that he will not stop fighting. He never felt so motivated to be alive.

He puts on his jeans and buttons his white shirt in front of the mirror. Then he looks at his reflection. His face does look pale and bloodless. He is wondering if the audience would notice. Maybe he should ask Michelle to put some makeup on his face. He grabs his hair gel and starts styling his hair. After he finishes, he walks into the bedroom and pulls out his suit for the concert tonight.

Black suit jacket, grey shirt, and black plants. That is the outfit he has selected for the last concert in New York. He cannot wait to see Gaby in her red dress. She will look stunning.

Suddenly his phone rings. It's Guillaume.

"*Allô* Guillaume. What's up?" André says.

"Raphael and I are in front of your suite. Can we come in?"

"Yes, for sure. Give me one sec."

André goes downstairs and opens the door. Guillaume and Raphael have worn their outfits to attend the concert. Guillaume is wearing a navy blue blazer jacket on top of his white shirt and Raphael wears a gray blazer jacket on top of his white shirt.

"Come in," André says. They both follow him to the penthouse suite. Both of them are examining his face.

"How are you feeling? You don't look very well," Guillaume comments.

"I am okay. It will be over in a few hours. I can survive."

"I cannot believe I'm letting you do this, André. This is very risky. You should be in the hospital right now," Raphael says.

"I'm fine, Raphael. As per your suggestion, I'll get checked tomorrow. I really appreciate your help. How's Gaby doing?"

"She looks worried. But I bet she is more worried about your condition than the concert."

"Ah, she always is."

"Michelle is helping Gaby with her make up. They will be done soon. Let's get ready," Raphael says.

Chapter 34

Saturday Evening
Carnegie Hall

They arrive at Carnegie Hall two and a half hours before the concert begins. Gaby and Michelle go directly into the audience at Stern Auditorium. Gaby will play the Aeolian Harp for the opening of session two. Therefore, she can enjoy session one from the audience seat. She looks at the program:

Chopin – Etude in C-Sharp minor Op. 10 No. 4 (Torrent)
Chopin – Etude in A minor Op. 25 No. 11 (Winter Wind)
Chopin – Piano Concerto No. 2 in F minor Op. 21:
Maestoso
Larghetto
Allegro Vivace

˜Intermezzo˜

Chopin – Etude in A-flat Major Op. 25 No. 1 (Aeolian Harp)
Chopin – Piano Concerto No. 1 in E minor Op. 11:
Allegro Maestoso
Romance Larghetto
Rondo Vivace

She really hopes that everything is fine with André and he can play everything well. André keeps saying that he is okay and he is just tired. But for some reasons, that does not put Gaby's mind at ease.

"Are you nervous, Gabs?" Michelle asks.

"Yes. There will be almost three thousand people this time. Also, I will be playing in front of the NYPO."

"That's a lot of pressure. But just be confident. Don't think about it as a concert. Just think about it as you are enjoying your own music. That's what I did whenever I did my solo part," Michelle says.

"Yes, I usually do that. Thanks, Michelle." Gaby forgets that Michelle also performs in public all the time. Thinking that everybody has gone through similar pre-performance stage fright makes Gaby feel calmer and accept her anxiety. This is a normal feeling for a performer, and she should get used to it. Even after performing twice, she is still nervous.

André has just changed into his suit when he suddenly feels dizzy. This time it is accompanied by a nauseous feeling in his stomach. His heart beats rapidly again and his vision starts to become blurry. 'Please, I cannot faint now,' André thinks. It is fifteen minutes before his performance.

Unfortunately, no matter how hard he tries to stay fully conscious, he feels like his legs can no longer support his body. He grabs the dressing table to prevent him from falling. Luckily, Raphael and Guillaume are also in the dressing room with him, and are able to support him.

"Let's lie him down on the floor," Raphael says to Guillaume. They lie André down on the floor and take off his jacket. Raphael can see that André is starting to lose consciousness. He has to act quickly.

"Guillaume, can you please get me my medical bag, call 911, and ask Gaby to come here as soon as possible?" Raphael instructs Guillaume. Guillaume nods and does everything Raphael says very quickly. He tries not to panic. He gives Raphael his medical bag and calls 911 right away.

Raphael quickly opens his medical bag and starts checking André's vitals. He measures André's blood pressure, temperature, oxygen saturation, and listens to his heart and lungs. Some vitals look alarming. His blood pressure is too low and his heart rate is too fast. The heart murmur he hears is as loud as the last time he examined him, but the carotid pulse is delayed and weak, which indicates that the aortic stenosis is getting worse. Raphael also hears fine crackles at the base of the lungs due to his congestive heart failure. André needs surgery soon. He will not be able to perform.

Guillaume comes back with Gaby and Michelle. Gaby is terrified when she looks at André lying down unconscious on the floor.

"Raphael! What happened?" Gaby quickly walks towards them.

"Gabs, get changed now. Get ready to perform while I am taking care of André. We need to buy some time. Michelle, please help Gaby," Raphael says. He is still kneeling on the floor beside André. He takes off his jacket too to put it under André's head to ease his breathing.

Michelle quickly helps Gaby get changed. Gaby feels like the next few minutes are just unreal. André's condition seems to worsen rapidly. She cannot think clearly right now.

"Gabs, stay focused. You are going to perform shortly okay? Are you ready?" Michelle asks her after she finishes dressing Gaby in her red gown.

Gaby nods. At least she can do this for André. Before she gets on stage, she kneels beside André and grabs his hand.

"André please, wake up. I am going to play shortly. Please stay conscious," Gaby says desperately. André seems to hear what Gaby says. He opens his eyes slowly. He seems disoriented at first. He tries to wake up but Raphael pushes his shoulder.

"Lie still. You just had a syncope." Raphael says.

Now André has become more alert. It looks like he has just fainted. He looks at Gaby's terrified face. Now he feels guilty. His fainting must have caused her to worry.

"Gaby, don't worry about me right now. Just give your best performance. I will be listening," André says with a hoarse and weak voice. He has pictured Gaby several times in her red dress. Now she is right here looking stunning in that dress.

"Yes, hang in there. I have to go now." Gaby quickly kisses him on the lips and leaves the room.

"Raphael, I think I feel better now. I need to get ready," André says.

"Please lie down for a few more minutes. I am going to take your blood pressure again. The EMS will arrive soon. They will bring you to the hospital. Don't think about the concert right now," Raphael says while he puts the blood pressure cuff around André's arm.

"But I have to finish my last concert," André protests.

Raphael looks at the result. It is still low but at least better. The oxygen level has also improved even though he is still breathing faster than normal. But Raphael is still uncertain of how bad is the aortic aneurysm right now. He has to make a judgement. How risky is it to let him perform? Raphael cannot decide. He examines André's face. It still looks pale but has more color than before.

"André, please. Your health is more important than the concert," Guillaume says.

"If I don't make it tonight, at least I'll finish my concert," André says.

Raphael looks very stressed. The decision is in his hands. André's heart condition is very unstable. What if the aneurysm dissects or ruptures? André can collapse at any moment and it may be fatal. But there is also the chance that he can survive for two hours and get the surgery right after the concert. But what if he does not survive within the next two hours? Before, they were counting days. Now, every hour counts.

"Raphael, I know what you are thinking. This is the risk I have to take. Please don't blame yourself if something happens to me. This is my decision," André says with determination. He gets up and tries to stand. When he does that, his heart races again. But this time he does not care. He has to finish his concert no matter what. He already promised Gaby.

He takes a deep breath, buttons up his shirt quickly, and puts on his jacket. He fixes his hair and looks at his reflection in the mirror. He still looks pale but he does not have time to care about that.

Raphael does not know what else to do. He cannot prevent André from performing. Guillaume looks like he has given up persuading André.

Three EMS paramedics finally appear at the door with a gurney, medical kit, defibrillator, and other emergency medical equipment. Raphael quickly informs them André's status and asks them to stand by.

Meanwhile, André starts walking towards the door. He wants to watch Gaby's performance. Raphael, Guillaume and the three paramedics have no choice but to follow behind him. When he reaches the backstage, Gaby is just bowing to the audience before she starts playing. The audience looks confused but still gives her applause. The orchestra is ready on their seats and also looks confused. Everyone is expecting him to be on stage by now. He has to give thumbs up to Gaby for her bravery to come up to the stage to fill in for him.

When Gaby starts playing her Aeolian Harp, André feels like time stops. He forgets that he has just fainted a few minutes ago. The way Gaby plays is very calming to his heart. Her hands are effortless and she plays with all her heart. André feels very lucky to be able to watch her like this. If something is going to happen to him, at least he has seen her perform in Carnegie Hall, in front of almost three thousand people.

Even though Gaby is on stage, she is not playing for the audience right now. She is playing for André. A picture of him lying on the floor unconscious is still in her head. But this time, she wants her music to keep him awake, to calm him, and to encourage him to be strong. She does not imagine herself playing piano. Instead she imagines herself playing a harp which has a calming effect. So she plays it softly in some parts and lively in other parts. She wants to tell André not to worry and that she will be beside him right away.

Her piece is only two minutes long, but she hopes that the impact will last much longer. When she finishes playing and bows, the audience gives her a big applause.

When she walks towards the backstage, she finds André standing there. She cannot describe how relieved she is. She hugs him tight. He hugs her back tightly.

"Thank you for your performance, Gaby. It gives me strength. Now, wish me luck," André says before walking towards the stage. The audience has already given him applause before he bows.

"Raphael, how is he doing?" Gaby asks her brother.

"He is... okay. For now." Raphael does not sound very sure.

Over the next forty minutes, Gaby, Michelle, Guillaume, Raphael, and the three paramedics enjoy André's performance from the backstage. They watch André closely in case he may collapse again. However, it turns out that André plays amazingly as usual. He plays Piano Concerto No. 2 first. Even though they cannot see his face from where they stand, André does not play like someone who has just fainted a few minutes ago. He plays the piece very beautifully. And his fingers are agile as usual.

Raphael is relieved that the syncope earlier does not affect André's motor skills nor his memory at all. André may have memorized the piece perfectly until he does not have to think about it anymore. It is one of the most intense forty minutes of Raphael's life. But hearing him playing with an orchestra right now makes him think that maybe André's condition is not as bad as he thinks? He really hopes that is the case.

Chapter 35

Saturday Evening
Carnegie Hall

During the intermezzo, they gather in the dressing room again. André still looks pale but other than that, he seems better than earlier.

The EMS team checks his vitals again while Raphael is busy making a call to his contact at the hospital to admit André approximately an hour from now, instead of tomorrow. Gaby has changed back to her blouse and jeans and returned to the dressing room. She never wants to leave André's side. The EMS team asks him to lie down on the gurney so that his heart does not have to work harder than necessary. The gurney is also tilted so that he can breathe easier.

"You guys performed really well. That was the first time I heard something like that. I don't know how you did it with your condition," one of the paramedics says to André and Gaby.

"Thanks," André and Gaby say in unison.

"Can you tell me what happened to you now? What condition do you have? Why are the paramedics here?" Gaby asks André.

"I will tell you later. You have performed really well Gaby. I am very proud of you. Thank you very much for everything you have done," André says and smiles. André does not want her to think about his condition right now. He wants her to free up her mind and heart to enjoy the last piece, Piano Concerto No. 1. He will tell her everything after his concert.

"Be strong for another forty minutes okay? For me, please."

"Yes, I promise," André says.

Then, it is time for André to get back on stage again. He gets up from the gurney and gets ready for session two. Gaby, Michelle, Raphael, and Guillaume will watch from the audience seats this time while the paramedics will stand by the backstage.

When Gaby finally sits in the audience seat, she feels her heart pounding with anxiety and excitement. She is more nervous in the audience than when she was on stage because she wants everything to go well for André. He has sacrificed a lot for this concert. And he will perform the most beautiful piece shortly.

Finally, André appears on the stage and he walks to the piano. The audience gives him a big applause and he bows. Everybody must notice that his face does not look well at all. But he still gives the audience his best smile. And then he starts playing the two Etudes before the Piano Concerto.

The Etudes that he chose for this concert are the two most difficult Etudes. The tempo is very fast and it requires a very strong technique. André plays them very impressively. The pieces give the audience both an adrenaline rush and chills. Even when his physical condition is not very good, he can play them very well. Gaby truly appreciates André's effort.

After that, it is time for their favourite piece: Piano Concerto No.1. The orchestra starts alone. They play very professionally and expressively. They are able to change the atmosphere in the hall between energetic and introspective on a dime. The orchestra has successfully made the audience get carried away emotionally. Now, everyone in the room is curious what André will say through his music.

Then, André starts playing. He is not only playing. He starts speaking through his music.

First, he speaks energetically and fast. Then, he recounts meaningful and sentimental moments in his life. Sometimes he sounds like he is in pain. He is asking why? There is a sense of desperation and disappointment. But other times, he sounds happy, joyful, and encouraging. There are also times when he looks like he is rushing, agitated, and angry. It is very complicated.

There is a mix of complex emotions in this piece, but André creates beautiful phrases in every up and down. What makes him a genius is that he does not treat each phrase separately; instead, he always connects one phrase to the next through a progressive dynamic. Therefore, the music flows really well. It does not feel like twenty minutes at all because the audience is curious what he will do next and what emotions he will display.

By the end of the first movement, everybody is already amazed and speechless.

Then, the second movement – Romance Larghetto – begins.

The mood is very different from the first movement. André is sharing a calm, relaxing, beautiful and sweet memory with everyone. The music flows beautifully. Gaby starts to reminisce about her sweet moments with André when they first met three weeks ago. From spilling coffee on him in Singapore, they then chatted about music and he asked her to perform with him.

Gaby does not know what to do without André. Without André, she would never be on these world-class stages. If she never experienced something like this, how would she truly appreciate the beauty of music, emotion, expression, love, and courage? Her life has been up and down since she met André. But because of him, she is able to explore herself and her emotions as a musician. She grows stronger through difficult times. She learns to love and to be loved. Getting to know André and performing with him are the best things that have ever happened in her life. André brings color to her life and brings out the best in her.

When the second movement ends, Gaby comes back from her daydreaming. The third movement begins.

Again, André keeps giving his audience surprises. The mood suddenly changes again. In this third movement, he plays it happily, fast, energetically, and even playfully. He displays similar emotion to when he performed in Auckland. For those who have followed André's musical career since he was a kid, like Gaby, they will know that this is a breakthrough in André's style. In the past, he never interpreted music like this. He usually performed a piece like this energetically and aggressively, but never happily and definitely not playfully. If Gaby only listens to the music without watching who the pianist is, she would not guess that it was André who was playing the piece.

What made his playing style change? Based on what she knows, throughout his life, André was always a serious, disciplined, and hardworking person. He also suffered loneliness due to his profession as a concert pianist. This life experience made him interpret virtuoso or sentimental pieces really well. However, as far as Gaby knows, André is not someone who enjoys life the way other people enjoy life. He started performing internationally when he was ten years old. He was not very social either. He never really had fun, or partied, or travelled with a group of friends, or went to a bar with co-workers after work.

Typically, a musical interpretation is drawn from one's own life experience. How could André play like this if he never truly experienced an emotion like this? Or, has he?

Gaby would assume that this is André's way of saying that he is going to live a happier life from now on. Gaby's mood also changes to become livelier and brighter. She hopes that she can do whatever she can to make André's life livelier and brighter from now on. She is really inspired by this Rondo Vivace, the third movement of the Piano Concerto.

André looks exhausted now. He is perspiring and breathing fast. However, it does not bother the audience. Rather, the audience takes it as he is being enthusiastic and they like it even more. The music that he produces also suggests that they are all in a happy and bright mood. So people are not actually aware that his physical condition is different from what the music suggests. Even Gaby, Raphael, Guillaume, and Michelle are so hypnotized by his music that they forget his physical condition is actually dangerous.

André is too focused on his performance. He does not even notice that he struggles to breathe. The music is like an anesthetic to his chest pain. If he was not in the middle of playing piano, he would have noticed that. But the problem is, he does not. His heart is beating faster and faster. His body demands more oxygen from his heart. At this rate, he can collapse at any moment. It is both a blessing and a curse that André is very immersed in his music. It is a blessing because he does not feel the pain. It is a curse because that pain itself is actually a warning that there is something wrong with his body.

Finally, he presses the last key.

He finishes his concert.

He has fulfilled his promise to Gaby. From the moment he started playing the Piano Concerto's first movement, everything was dedicated to and inspired by Gaby. The first movement represented his life before he met Gaby. It was up and down. But most of the time, he lived a stressful and sad life. There was a brief moment when he felt happy when he was with Charmaine. But it did not last long. His work and performance gave more pressure than the peace and comfort offered by Charmaine.

The second movement represented his life after he met Gaby. He felt calm and relaxed and at peace. He remembered every single sweet moment with Gaby. Her beautiful piano performance when he first met her in Singapore. Then, when she spilled coffee on his shirt. When she was afraid that would upset him, even though he actually felt lucky to find an excuse to keep her longer than necessary. There were a few times when Gaby confessed that she admired him and she was a fan of his. He found that that honesty was very adorable. She was brave enough to be vulnerable in front of him by confessing her admiration towards him. The more he got to know her, the more he adored her.

In Auckland, she showed him her toughness and persistence. She never gave up even when a spectator humiliated her. She stayed strong. He saw her crying the first time at Piha Beach. But they were not tears of pain. She was crying because she was touched emotionally by him. He never felt like he wanted to protect someone like that before.

In Geneva, she showed him her independence. She explored herself, her musical style, and her own emotions. He became more impressed with her music progress every day. They hugged and that was when he decided that he would be more honest with her and show her his feelings. After the concert that night, he could only show her his love and his care for her through a kiss.

Unfortunately, his heart condition got worse in New York. He wanted to express his love to Gaby even more. He wanted to be united with her. But his condition restricted him. Regardless, there was no doubt that he has fallen in love with her. Whenever she felt sick, anxious, or sad, he felt it too. Whenever she was happy, he too, was happy. To him, her life, her body, and her emotions are more important than his own.

The third movement represented his dream life with Gaby after this concert finished. He imagined it full of joy, enthusiasm, and fun moments. They will work hard and enjoy their fast-paced lives together.

The orchestra is currently finishing their last part. That is when André starts to become more aware of his physical condition. He suddenly feels an extreme pain in his chest that radiates towards his back and he realizes his struggle to breathe.

The orchestra finishes the last note and the audience rises to their feet to give them a standing ovation. Some of them shout bravo and other expressions of appreciation. André knows that it is his time to bow. This could be his last bow. Will he survive? Will this be his last concert? Is this what dying feels like?

With his last drops of energy, he rises up slowly while holding the piano to steady himself. He tries to find Gaby in the audience. There she is! He finds her in the second row with Guillaume, Raphael, and Michelle. They are all looking at him proudly.

He smiles at Gaby. I have fulfilled my promise. Now it's your turn. Be happy, whether it is being a concert pianist or not. Take care of yourself in case I cannot be around anymore.

I love you, Gaby...

He wishes he could say that out loud. But he can only speak through his eyes now. He hopes Gaby understands what he is trying to say. He can see that she nods at him and her eyes are full of tears.

He does not have much time anymore. His vision starts to blur again. He has no energy left in his body. His legs are unable to support him anymore. He tries to give one last bow, and then...

He collapses.

Chapter 36

Saturday Evening
Carnegie Hall – Columbia University Hospital

André seemed to say goodbye to her. She could feel that he was leaving her. At the same time, she feels that he loves her. Very deeply. It cannot be expressed in words. But they understand each other. Before Gaby could reply, he collapsed.

Gaby feels like time stops. Somehow, she can feel that André is not just fainting this time. It is more serious. Before she is able to react, Raphael quickly grabs his medical bag and runs towards the stage where André fell unconscious. The paramedic team that is standing by the backstage also runs towards him. She hears some of the spectators and orchestra members scream in shock. Still feeling like this is only a dream, she quickly rushes towards André with Michelle and Guillaume.

Raphael checks André's pulse. It is as he dreaded.

André has no pulse. He stops breathing.

He is in cardiac arrest.

Raphael quickly grabs scissors from the paramedic team and cuts André's shirt to expose his chest. He starts to perform CPR on André while the paramedic team prepares the AED.

Once the defibrillator is ready, one of the paramedics attaches the pads to André's chest while Raphael continues the CPR. The only time he stops is when the machine is analyzing the heart rhythm and instructs them to stand clear and deliver the shock.

They shock him a few times but there is still no pulse. Raphael continues the chest compression. He knows they should revive him in approximately five minutes. If within five minutes they cannot revive him, brain damage may occur.

Three minutes pass. Raphael starts to sweat but he does not give up. He also performs mouth-to mouth on André. Gaby is too shocked to process what happened. She cannot accept that André's heart has stopped. It means that he could leave her forever. 'Please don't,' she thinks. 'I still have so many things to say to you...'

Four minutes pass.

"I got a pulse!" Raphael says. He notices that André starts breathing again. They quickly carry him to the gurney and rush towards the ambulance. Gaby has never felt so hopeful in her life.

Gaby, Michelle, and Guillaume quickly follow. Guillaume calls a cab to follow the ambulance. But the ambulance needs to reach the hospital soon.

"We are going to Columbia University Irving Medical Center Milstein Hospital Building. I will meet you there," Raphael says before he gets into the ambulance with the paramedics.

Guillaume nods. Gaby and Michelle are still too shocked to react. Especially Gaby. She cannot believe that André's heart has stopped.

Finally the cab arrives. None of them says a word the whole ride. They don't know what the chances are that André will live. Although he has been resuscitated, does that mean he is safe now? Will he be alive?

Throughout his career as an emergency physician, this is the first time Raphael feels like a failure. He should not have let André delay the surgery for the sake of the concert. It was indeed a spectacular concert. He never watched something like that before. However, it was not worth it. Nothing is comparable to the worth of one's life. Raphael feels like he does not deserve to be a doctor at all. He has just failed his patient.

After they delivered André to the operating room for an emergency surgery, the paramedics looked as defeated as he did. Although they did not know André, they watched his concert, too. They were all touched by his extraordinary performance. Even a lay person who is not really familiar with classical music knows what a genius pianist André is.

The paramedics have left, as they have to return to their post. Raphael is sitting in the waiting area by himself. He is waiting for Gaby, Michelle, and Guillaume to arrive. He does not know if he can bear this by himself anymore.

He sees Gaby, Michelle, and Guillaume coming towards him. Their faces look very worried.

"Raphael, how's André?" Gaby asks.

"He is in the operating room right now," Raphael answers without enthusiasm.

"Do you know how long the surgery will be?" Michelle asks.

"Seven or eight hours maybe."

"Is it an open heart surgery?" Guillaume asks. Raphael just nods.

"What are his chances?" Gaby asks carefully.

Raphael does not know how to answer that. He cannot bear this anymore. He feels tears in his eyes. It's been a while since he cried. The last time he cried was probably in elementary school. He does not want to face Gaby or anyone else at this point. He suddenly feels nauseous, and he quickly runs towards the bathroom.

Once in the bathroom, he goes into one of the booths and throws up in the toilet. Once he finishes throwing up, he flushes the toilet. He feels very tired, powerless, and guilty. He leans his head towards the wall and inhales deeply.

Raphael never considers himself as an emotional person. He is more logical than emotional, especially at work where it was such a fast-paced environment and he had to multitask and treated multiple patients at the same time. There was just no time for being emotional. And today was not the first time he had to deal with cardiac arrest.

But André is a special case. He is not a patient. He is a genuine and sincere person who loves Gaby deeply and always puts Gaby first before himself. Raphael feels very sad for Gaby. He had never love someone like the way André loves Gaby. In a short period of time, André has truly inspired him through his love for Gaby and his touching piano performances. Raphael doesn't want to lose this person.

"Raphael? Are you there?" He hears Guillaume's voice.

"Yes I am here. Give me a sec." He rubs his eyes with his shirt's sleeve. He doesn't want anyone to see him in this state. Once he feels better, he comes out.

Guillaume is standing there. Raphael cannot read his face.

"Guillaume, I am so sorry," Raphael starts. He does not know how to apologize, how to express his regret, and what else to say.

"Hey, I am the one who should be thankful. You have saved André's life. We are forever grateful to you!" Guillaume says. Raphael is impressed that Guillaume is taking this situation more calmly than he is.

"No. You are wrong. I did not save André's life. I am the one who should be blamed for this."

"What are you talking about? You did everything you could! You performed CPR on him, you revived him, you made a correct judgement by telling me to call the EMS earlier. You brought him here right on time. What else could you do, Raphael?"

"I was not supposed to let him finish the concert. The moment I knew something was wrong with his heart, I should have brought him to the operating room."

"Okay, what about me then? I found out about his condition even before this concert began. You barely know André and you are not even his physician."

Raphael does not answer. So Guillaume continues, "Raphael, listen. There is something you should know." He pauses. Raphael quickly raises his head to face Guillaume.

"When André found out that his condition was getting worse, he never intended to make it."

"What do you mean?"

"He knew that he had to have a surgery in order to survive. But he refused. That was why he announced his retirement. He did not have any motivation to live anymore. But then, suddenly he changed his mind..." Guillaume explains. Raphael does not need to ask Guillaume why André would change his mind. He knows the answer.

"I tried to change his mind, but I failed. But you have saved him, Raphael. I cannot be more thankful to you. André is like my own brother," Guillaume says.

'I look forward to becoming brothers with André too – if he is alive and he continues to make Gaby happy.' Raphael thinks. He cannot bear this thought anymore. He starts to cry. He covers his eyes with his hand. Guillaume hugs him and lets him cry on his shoulder.

"Guillaume," Raphael says on his shoulder. "I don't want you to lose your hope. However, staying alive after the resuscitation itself was already a miracle. There is a very high chance that he will not make it."

Chapter 37

Saturday Evening – Sunday Morning
Columbia University Hospital

Gaby cannot just sit there and think about all the worst possible scenarios for André. She walks back and forth nervously. If something happens with André in the operating room, she would feel it right? Michelle's face does not look good either. She sits and does some research on her phone about heart surgery and the survival rate. Although Michelle interacted with André less than Gaby and Raphael, they have started to become friends too. She wants André to survive as badly as everybody else.

"I don't like waiting like this when we don't even know the chances. Why didn't Raphael tell us?" Michelle complains to Gaby. Gaby stops walking and takes a seat beside Michelle. She knows that the reason Raphael did not tell them is because the chances are low.

"Let's just hope for a miracle." Gaby sighs.

Not long after, Raphael and Guillaume appear and walk towards them. Raphael looks a bit better. Guillaume looks like he already accepts everything that may happen. Gaby decides that it is the time for her to know everything.

"Raphael, could you tell me now what André's illness is? I have been kept in the dark all this time. I know it was because you guys didn't want me to be distracted from the concert. But now that the concert is over, I have the right to know, right?" Gaby says. Raphael looks at her with his red eyes after throwing up and crying.

"He has a congenital heart condition named bicuspid aortic valve."

"What's that supposed to mean?" Michelle asks. Raphael explains.

"Normal people have an aortic valve with three cusps. But André's aortic valve only has two cusps. That makes it harder for his heart to pump blood to the rest of his body. He did not display symptoms in his early life. The symptoms only became apparent lately. Unfortunately, when I first found out about this, his heart condition was already progressing to severe aortic stenosis, heart failure, and aortic aneurysm. That is why he was having all those symptoms like chest pain, difficulty breathing, irregular heartbeat, palpitations, dizziness, and fainting."

Now it all makes sense to Gaby. She knew that something was wrong with André. It is hard to believe that someone young and fit like him could suffer from a heart disease.

"Raphael, tell us, what are the chances of him surviving?" Gaby asks.

"I searched up heart surgery, and what I found was the survival rate is quite high," Michelle adds.

"It is not high when cardiac arrest has happened. The chances are lower."

"How low?"

"Extremely low. We have to be ready," Raphael says weakly. Nobody says anything for a while. Gaby feels like someone has just hit her stomach.

"If he had the surgery earlier, would he have had a higher chance?" Gaby asks.

"Yes. I am really sorry Gaby," Raphael answers.

"No. This is my fault. André insisted on performing until the last minute because of me. He wanted me to perform and he wanted to perform that last Piano Concerto because it is my favourite piece. He could have just cancelled his concert if I took no part in his concert."

"That's not true Gaby. This is my fault..." Guillaume starts.

"No, this is my fault..." Raphael says.

"Okay stop." Michelle cannot bear to hear this anymore. "There is no point in blaming yourselves now. It happened. Now, let's think about the future instead of the past. Like, is there anything we can do at this point? Only the surgeons can make a difference now. We cannot do anything," Michelle says wisely.

"That's true," Raphael says.

They sit in silence again. It is already two in the morning. They are all exhausted. They don't know when the surgery will end.

Although Gaby has only known André for three weeks, she feels like she cannot live without him. She cannot imagine her life without him. Extremely low chance? Does that mean she has to be ready now? 'No. He will be fine,' Gaby thinks. 'I can feel it.'

If André did not make it, she would not be able to listen to his beautiful live performance anymore, she would never hear his laugh nor see his smile anymore, she would never be able to hold his hand or hug him anymore. And who would give her feedback about her piano performance and support her when she was feeling down? How would she feel when she listened to his albums if he was not there anymore? How would she feel every time she played Chopin's music? How would she continue playing piano without thinking about him?

What if they never have a chance to speak to each other again? She has so many things to say to him. She has not said, I love you...

Suddenly Gaby cannot hold her tears anymore. Her throat hurts from holding them back. She finally lets herself sob. Raphael holds her shoulders and lets her cry into his chest. She sheds a lot of tears until Raphael's shirt is wet.

Gaby never felt this sad. She suddenly feels hopeless. She and André have just begun their relationship. Why does it have to end that fast? She hasn't had enough time to make him happy, to cheer him up when he was stressed, to be there for him when he was lonely, and to support him they way he supported her.

Meanwhile, Michelle holds Guillaume's hand. She knows that Guillaume must be the most vulnerable among them all. Guillaume has known André for such a long time and they are like brothers. Michelle cannot imagine if something bad happened to Raphael or Gaby. Although Guillaume is not a very expressive person, Michelle can feel that today he is more tense and distressed. He is just really good at keeping it to himself.

Guillaume has prepared for a time like this. He knew André's condition since before the tour began. He was shocked at the time. He was also angry at André who did not want to fight harder for his life. What was lacking in André's life? He had everything. Also, did he mean nothing to André? But the more Guillaume analyzed it, the more he realized that André was not completely unreasonable to give up on his life. Yes, he has tons of money, he is very popular, he owns a firm, and he is a piano prodigy. From an outsider's perspective, who does not want a perfect life like that?

But the more he thinks about André's life, the more he understands. What André needs in his life is pure and unconditional love. The audience loves him because of his piano performance. Many girls chase him because he has money. But he wants to feel loved for who he is, not because he is a pianist or a firm owner. He wants to be himself. But no one has ever given him pure love since his parents died six years ago. Guillaume himself would stick to André even if André was no one. But eventually, Guillaume would have a family of his own. André explained to him that when that time came, André would see no reason to live, as he has no one else he can take care of. Why push forward with the surgery just to feel empty again once he resumes his normal life? He was tired of living. He felt empty and unmotivated. He did not see the point of giving performances anymore. Until he met Gaby...

Everyone in the operating room is nervous. They are performing a composite aortic root replacement. The patient is still young. He is a twenty-nine year-old male and fit. The imaging showed an aortic dissection, which was where the inner layer of the aorta teared and caused the inner and middle layer of the aorta to dissect. If this is a normal aortic valve and aortic root replacement, it is supposed to be a high survival rate surgery. However, the patient was brought in a bit too late, the ascending aorta has dissected and the patient has had cardiac arrest earlier. This makes the survival rate extremely low. However, they perform the surgery anyway.

Dr. Bernstein, a fifty-year-old experienced cardiothoracic surgeon is performing the surgery. He is someone who does not give up easily, even if the survival rate is extremely low. The patient's heart has been stopped and connected to a heart lung machine. The ascending aorta has been replaced with a graft as well. Dr. Bernstein is currently replacing the patient's aortic valve. The patient's aortic valve only has two cusps, while normal people have three. This makes the patient suffer from aortic valve stenosis as well. This is a very complex surgery, but Dr. Bernstein and his surgery team have done very well so far.

After Dr. Bernstein finishes replacing the aortic valve, it is time to stop the heart and lung machine and let the patient's heart beat on its own. All the surgery team is nervous including Dr. Bernstein. Will the heart be able to beat again?

*

It's almost five in the morning and the surgery is not over yet. Gaby takes it as a good sign. If the surgeons come out from the operating room too quickly, that would be a bad sign, right? She waits patiently. So do Raphael, Michelle, and Guillaume. None of them falls asleep even one second. Everybody is nervous and tired.

"Gaby, can I talk to you for a second?" Guillaume says. Gaby is a bit confused but she nods.

"Let's take a walk," Gaby suggests. They walk towards a more private area by the window. Guillaume remains silent for the first five minutes. He does not know where to start.

"Gaby, I just want to say thank you." Guillaume starts.

"To me? For what?"

"I think you should know this. As Raphael has said, André has known for a long time that he has a heart problem. When he felt that his condition was worsening and his doctor told him that he needed surgery, he never intended to get surgery."

"Wait, what do you mean? He wanted to give up?"

"Yes."

"But Raphael said that the surgery had high survival rate if he did not have cardiac arrest. Why would he give up?"

"Because he had no motivation to live."

Gaby does not say anything at first. She is trying to digest what Guillaume has just said.

"I can understand him. And I don't blame him. He has lived a stressful life since he was young. He always shares his music with the audience, but he has no one to share love with since Charmaine left him," Gaby says. Guillaume looks at Gaby closer. How does she, who has only known André for three weeks know that? While Guillaume, who has known André for six years, did not realize it until just now.

"Did he tell you that?"

"No. But I can guess it from the way he plays his music," Gaby says.

"He had no motivation to live, until he met you, Gaby," Guillaume says. Gaby looks at him with a surprised expression.

"After he spent some time with you, he decided to get the surgery and continue his life after the tour. I am glad that you entered into his life. It seems that he finally found someone who can share both love and music with him."

*

Dr. Bernstein and the rest of the surgical team come out of the operating room as Guillaume and Gaby return to the waiting area. Raphael and Michelle quickly approach Dr. Bernstein.

"The operation went well. But his condition is very critical. The next thirty days will be very important," Dr. Bernstein says. Gaby, Michelle, and Guillaume sigh with relief and hug each other. Only Raphael does not look very relieved. The doctor himself does not seem very enthusiastic either, although he has just finished a very complex surgery with a very low survival rate.

"Thank you doctor. You did your best," Raphael says.

"You are welcome. We will move him to the cardiac ICU now," Dr. Bernstein says before leaving.

"Raphael! Does that mean that André has beaten the odds? That extremely low chance really happened!" Michelle cries.

Raphael does not want to ruin their happiness, but he knows that André's fight is not over yet. Most patients die not during the surgery but typically within thirty days after the surgery. That is why Dr. Bernstein did not look very happy, even though the surgery was a success.

Chapter 38

Sunday
Columbia University Hospital

Three hours after the operation finished, they are finally able to visit André in the cardiac ICU. When Gaby first sees him, she cannot bear to see him in that condition. There is so many equipment attached to his body. His mouth is attached to an endotracheal tube and he is breathing through a ventilator. There are tubes attached to his chest as well as several electrodes that connect to a heart monitor. The incision on his chest is bandaged. His arm is connected to an IV. There are various monitors showing his vital signs.

Gaby cannot hold her tears. Seeing him very vulnerable like this is painful for her. André looks like he is barely alive. Will his life go back to normal again? Can he play piano again? For Gaby, it does not matter whether he can live a normal life or not after this. She will still love him no matter what. Gaby just doesn't want to see André in pain.

"Raphael, is he in pain right now?" Gaby asks.

"No, he is still under anesthetic. But after the anesthetic wears off, the chest incision may hurt, but he will be on painkillers. Don't worry. The doctors and nurses know what they are doing."

"When will he wake up?" Guillaume asks.

"Anytime now, once the anesthetic wears off," Raphael answers. Raphael believes in André. He knows that André is tough. His body may not be strong, but his will to live is strong. The fact that André is still alive after experiencing cardiac arrest and eight hours of tough surgery shows that he is fighting hard. Technically his heart has stopped twice, once during the cardiac arrest, and another time when the doctors put him on a heart-lung machine. Raphael is extremely proud of him and hopeful.

"Gaby, when he wakes up, say whatever you want to say to him. Do what you want to do with him. His condition will still be unstable after he wakes up. In case the worst-case scenario happens, at least we will have done all we could. I am just giving you a heads up. I believe with moral support and care from you, he will be able to go through this," Raphael says.

Gaby nods. She has to be ready but she will do whatever she can to keep him alive. The message from Raphael is clear. Although the surgery was a success, it does not guarantee that André will survive. She does not want to lose hope, but at the same time, she has to be ready.

They wait nervously for André to wake up.

*

André finally opens his eyes. At first, his vision is blurred and he does not know where he is. Slowly but surely, he regains consciousness. He can see the white ceiling and the lamp. He realizes that he is in a hospital gown and he is lying in a hospital bed. He cannot move because he has no energy to move and it looks like his body is attached to so many tubes. He feels like someone is pushing his chest and it feels heavy. He cannot speak either because there is something inside his mouth and throat. The feeling is weird and surreal.

He tries to remember how he got there. He remembers he played his last piece at the concert. He was relieved that he was able to finish it. Then he remembers looking directly at Gaby in the audience. After that, he does not remember anything. How long ago was that? What day is it today?

Suddenly he hears Gaby's voice and she appears in front of him. Her eyes look worried but very happy. She grabs his hand. Although he is still a bit disoriented, he is aware of her presence.

"André! Can you hear me? Do not try to speak and don't move, I will call a doctor."

André starts to be able to digest what happened. He is alive! And Gaby is here with him. Did they just perform a surgery on him? Is that why his chest feels heavy and weird? If he is still alive, does that mean he can be beside Gaby forever?

André looks at Gaby's face closely. Her eyes are red. She looks like she has cried a lot and is very tired. André wonders if she has slept. When her face becomes clearer to him, he feels at peace. He forgets about the pain in his body and all the equipment attached to it. Looking at Gaby can cure anything.

His heart monitor seems to beep faster as he wakes up and is excited to find Gaby there beside him. Gaby looks panicked for a second and looks at the door hoping that the doctor will come soon.

André does not want her to panic. He squeezes her hand weakly. She turns her head back towards him. He wants to say "I am okay, don't worry," to her, but because he cannot smile or say anything, he nods slowly while squeezing her hand again. He hopes that this will convey what he wants to say to her.

She understands his gesture very quickly and smiles. "Raphael, Michelle, and Guillaume are downstairs. They are getting breakfast. They will come here soon and they will be very happy to see you already awake." Gaby says.

"André, you are very strong. Thank you for staying alive. Please continue to be strong. I want to spend more time with you. These past three weeks felt like a dream to me. I would never imagine myself being able to talk to you heart-to-heart, listening to your piano practice, practicing together with you, playing piano in front of you, and loving you. I never felt like this before. I have never felt so loved and protected.

"After you played the Piano Concerto No. 1, I made a firm decision. I will enroll in a music program. I want to be able to touch people's hearts with my music and inspire them just like you did. I want to play piano more for you. But you have to survive okay? Otherwise, how would you be able to listen to my music? I will practice hard so that I can make you happy. But if you don't survive, I will stop playing piano forever.

"André, you have always been protective towards me. Now it is my turn. I will take care of you and protect you. Don't worry about anything else. Don't think about piano or work right now. Just think about getting better. I don't care if you can play piano again after this or not. It does not matter for me, because...I love you the way you are, André." She squeezes his hand and kisses it gently.

André sees Gaby's tears. He cannot believe what he is hearing. This is the first time he hears her saying that she loves him. And she loves him the way he is. Even if he is lying on the hospital bed powerlessly like this, she still loves him and accepts him. He feels her sincerity. He too, never felt loved and protected like this. He is frustrated that he cannot speak right now. He wants to tell Gaby that he loves her too. He has been wanting to say this a long time, but he restrained himself because he was not sure he would survive. He didn't want Gaby to fall in love with a dying man. But now that he is alive, he has the right to love Gaby.

Although he cannot speak, Gaby always understands his thoughts and feelings without him telling her. She can read his mind because she always listens to his music. She knows him very well. Therefore, André just nods to give the message that he understands. He feels very touched by Gaby. He suddenly feels tears in his eyes too. He tries to control his emotion, as he cannot let himself cry right now while he is breathing through a ventilator. He slowly and carefully raises his hand, which is still squeezing Gaby's hand, to his cheek. His hand still feels very weak and every movement in his arm makes his chest hurt slightly, but finally he can feel Gaby's hand on his cheek. He feels very calm.

Gaby wipes the tears from his face.

Chapter 39

Eight months later...
August
Koerner Hall, Toronto

André, Guillaume, Raphael, and Michelle are sitting in the audience at Koerner Hall. The concert is about to begin and they are very excited.

Gaby appears on stage and walks gracefully towards the piano. She wears a long peach dress. She looks very beautiful and professional. She smiles and bows to the audience. The audience gives her a welcome applause and then she starts to play.

Chopin's Nocturne in C minor Op. 48 No. 1.

André is absorbing the melody. It is very calming and relaxing for the first half of the piece. But then it becomes dramatic for the last half. Gaby plays it very well. There are some challenging parts but she plays them smoothly and effortlessly. Every time André listens to her perform, she always surprises him, whether it is with an improved technique or interpretation. He could not be happier.

André feels more than lucky to be alive. He was never able to express his gratitude to Gaby, Raphael, Guillaume, and Michelle. They all contributed to his fast recovery post surgery. After the surgery, he stayed at Columbia University for a month until the end of January. Throughout that time, Gaby and Guillaume were always beside him. Gaby decided to take a one-year sabbatical from her accounting firm. She was supposed to go back to work in early January, but she decided to stay with André in New York.

André's recovery after the surgery was not as bad as he thought it would be. Yes, the surgical incision on his chest was painful whenever he moved. He had to move very carefully. He also had to do deep breathing and coughing exercises, and a physiotherapist taught him how to pull and push himself from the bed without hurting his chest. However, every time he felt the pain, he always reminded himself that feeling pain meant he was still alive and he should be grateful. Raphael said that he had beaten the odds.

Gaby was very supportive. She was the reason he got through it. She went back and forth between the hospital and The Plaza to visit him. Whenever she went back to the hospital from The Plaza, she always showed him new video recordings of her playing the piano. That had a huge impact on him. He felt less anxious and more positive during his recovery. He could sleep better at night too.

Once he was discharged, they went back to his condo in Montreal and Gaby came along. That was one of the happiest moments in André's life despite his chest wound. His condo was no longer empty. Gaby stayed there with him and played piano for him all the time. Guillaume also stayed there a lot. Raphael and Michelle also visited a couple times. In Montreal, André and Gaby often took a walk along the Old Port. The doctor recommended that André take a short walk every day for his recovery.

Initially, he did not let Gaby see the surgery wound on his chest. Even to him, the wound looked nasty. It was six inches long, and in the beginning, it was swollen, slightly red, bumpy, and sometimes discharged clear fluids. But Gaby insisted on helping him change his dressing. She did not even flinch the first time she saw it. André really appreciated that. He felt like a damaged good with the surgery wound that would not disappear from his chest. But Gaby didn't care. She loves him and she accepts him the way he is.

André did not play piano for the first three months after the surgery. But he was fine with it because Gaby was always there playing piano for him. He tried to catch up with work and he was relieved that there was nothing much he could do. The IPO for the Tech Company went very well. All the outstanding shares were sold. Gauthier Capital made a significant profit. André couldn't be happier.

They stayed in Montreal until the end of April. At that time, André's condition had gotten better. Although he still experienced shortness of breath sometimes, there was no more fainting, dizziness, and fatigue. Overall, he felt much stronger and he could climb the stairs easily, unlike before.

André didn't want to hold Gaby back from her family and life in Toronto. So, he decided to move to Toronto temporarily. Guillaume assisted him in buying a three-bedroom condo at the Shangri-La Residence. André asked Gaby to move in with him and she agreed. Now that they live in Toronto, Raphael and Michelle can visit and even stay over at his place too. André and Guillaume also met Gaby, Raphael, and Michelle's parents when they were invited for a dinner at their residence in the North York area. André felt so happy to have a family again. Guillaume and Michelle have also been dating seriously since the concert. He couldn't be happier.

Right after they settled in Toronto, Gaby enrolled in a music school as she promised. She practiced hard for the audition and was accepted at The Glenn Gould School for their BMus program. André was very proud of her.

Now they are all enjoying her performance, as the school requires all their students to give student recitals and community performances. When Gaby finishes her Nocturne, the audience gives her a big applause. She continues to play more of Chopin's pieces. It feels to André like a dream, being able to watch her like this. It has not even been a year since they first performed together in Auckland. Now, she looks much more confident. André did not miss performing for public. He is not even sure he still wants to give concerts. He would rather just focus on guiding Gaby to become a professional pianist.

When he is not working, he spends his time volunteering at a local hospice, giving a free performance to the terminally ill patients there. Surprisingly, he feels that his life is more meaningful doing this. As someone who has experienced the brink of death himself, he can relate to these people. Rather than being a concert pianist, he is much happier and satisfied helping someone to become a concert pianist and letting his music bring joy to people who are enjoying their last moments of life. Luckily, he still can play piano as well as before the surgery. Therefore, anytime he wants to come back to being a concert pianist, he can. Although, that probably won't be in the near future.

Gaby bows to the audience after she finishes her last piece. She looks at André who is giving her a standing applause among the audience. She knows exactly where he sits. Raphael, Michelle, and Guillaume are also there with him giving her applause. She would not be as happy and as satisfied as now if they were not there supporting her. Gaby could not imagine being André, who most of the time knew no one in the audience other than Guillaume. It must have been super lonely. Her parents unfortunately cannot make it today as her dad was invited to a lawyers' networking event and her mom had to accompany her dad. But they always came to her other recitals in the past. So, she is not very disappointed today.

After the concert finishes, Gaby goes back to the backstage to get changed. Overall, she feels good about how she played in the concert today. There were some parts she was not satisfied with but at least she had practiced as much as she could and she had done her best. Therefore, there was no regret. After she gets back to her blouse and jeans, she finds André, Guillaume, Raphael, and Michelle outside the dressing room. They will celebrate her after-concert at a Japanese restaurant in Yorkville.

*

As they eat, Gaby observes André quietly. She is very happy that he has gotten back his appetite. A few weeks after the surgery, he lost weight because he had no appetite. The doctor said it is very common. But now he eats like normal again.

"Are you okay, Gaby?" André brings her back from her reverie.

"Oh, yes," Gaby says quickly. "Do you like the food?"

"Yes. This is the best." He puts a piece of sushi in his mouth. He seems to enjoy the food.

"Good."

"So Gaby, are you going to be a professional pianist for the rest of your life then? What about your accounting career?" Guillaume asks.

"Good question. Right now, I will focus on my piano education first. If it does not work out well, I can always go back to accounting," Gaby answers.

"It will work out well. I know it," André says with a smile.

"Yeah, I have confidence in you too, Gabs. You have always been listening to classical music and playing piano since you were young. It shows that this is your passion. You should pursue it. And you have made significant progress over the past few months. Even I, someone who does not quite understand classical music, can tell the difference," Raphael says.

"Thanks Raphael. Are you going to start taking piano lessons now?" Gaby asks.

"No. I am too old. I will just enjoy listening to you."

"I am glad that finally my sister decided to become a performing artist too!" Michelle adds.

"We'll see. Wish me luck, Michelle," Gaby says.

"When you become a professional, Guillaume can be your manager too," André says. Guillaume smiles and nods encouragingly.

Chapter 40

The Shangri-La Residence
Toronto

André is enjoying the night view of Toronto from his penthouse, facing west. He can see the CN Tower. Tonight is very calm and peaceful. The lights are very beautiful. But he will miss Gaby tonight. Gaby is staying at her parents' in North York as her parents requested. They want to inquire after her about the concert. André really likes that she is close to her parents. He likes a family-oriented woman as he does not have a family himself.

Suddenly he hears a knock on his door. It must be Guillaume. He agreed to stay with him tonight. André opens the door and finds Guillaume there.

They catch up about life for a while. Now that both André and Guillaume are in a relationship, it's been a while since they had the chance to talk one-on-one like this. Guillaume has recently bought a place near the harbour front with Michelle. They live there together.

"How's your surgery scar? Can I see?" Guillaume asks.

André hesitates at first. But then he says, "yeah sure." He unbuttons the first few buttons of his white shirt to show Guillaume his scar.

"That looks much better than last time. It does not hurt anymore, does it?" Guillaume asks.

"Nope. And thank you for taking care of me after the surgery. It meant a lot, Guillaume. I did not know what to do without you." André buttons up his shirt.

"I didn't do much. It was mostly Gaby all the time."

"At least you guys took turns and both of you had a chance to rest."

"That's true. I am so glad that Gaby was there. How is it going between you two?"

"Tell me first, how is it going with Michelle?"

"It's been great, you know. I really enjoy living with her. It feels like we are married already."

"Glad to hear. Remember last time when I said I had no motivation to continue living even for you, because you will eventually get married and forget about me anyway. And you did not believe that. Look at you now."

"Well, I am still pissed off, you know. I thought I was worth more to you, and that you would be willing to get surgery for me. Although I am with Michelle now, I won't forget you. You are the one who is busy with Gaby."

"That's true. I feel glad that I am able to live now. Our lives are so great."

"Yeah. How is it going with you and Gaby?" Guillaume asks.

"Well, I have good news for you."

*

The next morning, André is nervous waiting for Gaby. He has a big plan for her today. But he is not sure how she will take it. He remembers his conversation with Raphael a few days ago when he told Raphael his plan.

"That's great André! I fully support you!" Raphael said when he visited André at his place. Raphael is working at a hospital that is within walking distance from the Shangri-La, on University Ave. Raphael often stops by to check in on him. André is forever grateful to Raphael. Raphael always reminded him about the dietary restrictions and the exercise limitations; as well as reminding him to take his medications and to clean his surgical wound. Even though André had a family doctor and a cardiologist in Toronto, Raphael was still his go-to person when he had a quick medical question related to his post-surgery condition.

"You really don't mind?"

"Why would I?"

"Well, you know my condition."

"You are as alive as everybody else."

"But I am on medications for the rest of my life. I have to get a check-up every three months. And there could be complications in the future. I am not worthy of Gaby, Raphael. My heart is full of artificial materials. I feel like a damaged good. And the scar will never fade away, will it?"

"André, listen. You are not perfect. And neither is Gaby. But that's what makes you two a perfect couple. She will take care of you and you will take care of her. You guys need each other," Raphael said. André was digesting Raphael's words. He didn't know how to respond. What Raphael said was true.

"Don't worry about your scar. It will be less noticeable over time. And you will get used to it. It is part of your body now. It will remind you how strong you are after what you have been through. You should be proud of yourself, André."

"Thanks, Raphael. I really appreciate it."

"And the reason you fought hard was for Gaby right?" Raphael asked. André nodded.

"Then what are you waiting for? Why are you still hesitating?"

André comes back from his reverie. He sits on the piano bench in his living room, opens a box in his hand, and looks at the ring closely. Gaby does not like to be flashy. She likes something nice and sweet. So, he bought the prettiest ring, not necessarily the most expensive with the biggest diamond.

Suddenly, André hears the door open. He quickly puts the box into his pocket. That must be Gaby. Only Gaby has a spare key to his residence.

"Hi André!" Gaby walks towards him and kisses his cheek.

"How was your night at your parents?"

"It was great. They regretted that they could not make it, but I said it was fine. The party was very important for dad's business. And they have heard me playing piano throughout my life. Not attending one concert was no big deal."

"They are very lucky to have such an understanding daughter."

Gaby laughs, and walks towards the giant floor to ceiling window to enjoy the Toronto morning view from the 60th floor. André is suddenly nervous. He rises from the piano and stands behind Gaby. This is the time. He will do it now. She will accept it, won't she?

"Gaby, I have something to ask you," André stutters. Although he used to be a professional pianist who performed all over the world, right now he feels like he cannot do what he is supposed to. How do they do it so smoothly and perfectly in the movies?

"What is it?" Gaby turns to face him.

"I..." He decides to get down to one knee. He takes out the box from his pocket and opens it. Gaby is very surprised.

"André..."

"Gaby, I know that I am not perfect. I am not as healthy as other guys. I don't know if I could continue my career as a pianist. I am very broken. Forgive my selfishness, but, I would like to spend the rest of my life with you. I will try to be healthier so that I can take care of you. I want to make you happy even though I am like this. Will you marry me?" He raises his head to look up to her with so much hope.

Gaby kneels down so that she is at the same level as André. She puts both her hands on his face.

"André, listen. Do not ever think that you are imperfect because of your heart condition. In fact, you have a sincere and brave heart. I will never love you less because of your condition. I even love you more. The more you show your vulnerability, the more I want to take care of you."

"Thanks Gaby. Is that a yes?" He smiles.

"Yes. Absolutely, yes." She gives him her hand. André has never felt as happy as he does in this moment. He puts the ring on Gaby's finger and helps her stand.

They look at each other, smile, and hug each other tight.

The Romance Concerto has not finished. It has just begun.